Nicholas Moonlight

Also by Eileen Dunlop

The Haunting of Alice Fairlie
The Ghost by the Sea
Ghoul's Den
Warrior's Bride
Tales of St Columba

Nicholas Moonlight

Eileen Dunlop

POOLBEG
FOR CHILDREN

This novel is entirely a work of fiction. The names,
characters and incidents portrayed in it are the work of the
author's imagination. Any resemblance to actual persons,
living or dead, events or localities is entirely coincidental.

Published 2002
by Poolbeg Press Ltd.
123 Grange Hill, Baldoyle
Dublin 13, Ireland
Email: poolbeg@poolbeg.com

13579108642

A catalogue record for this book is available from the British Library.

ISBN 1 84223 058 1

Cover design by Steven Hope
Cover illustration by Jackie Lawler
Typeset by Patricia Hope in Goudy 11.5/16
Printed by Cox & Wyman

www.poolbeg.com

About the Author

Eileen Dunlop was born and went to school in Alloa, Clackmannanshire, Scotland, near where she now lives. She has published a number of novels for children, of which *The House on the Hill* (1987) was commended for the Carnagie Medal, *Finn's Island* (1991) commended for the McVitie's Prize for the Scottish Writer of the Year and *The Maze St* (1982) and *Clementina* (1985) won Scottish Arts Council Books Awards.

She has also, with her husband Antony Kamm, written several information books on Scottish themes, and compiled two collections of verse. She is the author of *Tales of St Patrick*, *Tales of St Columba*, *Stones of Destiny*, *Waters of Life*, *The Ghost by the Sea*, *Warrior's Bride*, *Ghoul's Den* and *The Haunting of Alice Fairlie* all published by Poolbeg, and has contributed short stories to three horror anthologies: *Shiver*, *Chiller* and *Nightmares*, also published by Poolbeg. *Ghoul's Den* was shortlisted for the RAI awards in 2001.

For Bob Cowan

Contents

1

The Shadow on the Pier

The first night on Seagull Island, I couldn't get to sleep. It wasn't because a high, full moon was shining in at the uncurtained window, throwing grey, truncated shadows across the floor. I wasn't a moon lover, for reasons that will become clear, but moonlight had never frightened me. It wasn't even because the bed was freezing, not having been slept in for months; the hot-water bottle Dad had filled had gone cold in twenty minutes and my toes felt like ten ice lollies. The reason I couldn't sleep was that I was spooked. Earlier in the day, I'd seen a shadow that wasn't attached to a body.

"Oh, don't be daft," Dad had said when I told him during supper. O D-OA-N-T B-EE D-A-F-T. "It must have been a trick of light." A T-R-I-K O-V L-AY-T.

I couldn't be bothered arguing, but I knew he was

1

wrong. I washed down the last of my sausage and egg with Coke, left the table and went upstairs to get ready for bed. I was totally pooped but I knew, as I put the light out, that I wouldn't be able to sleep.

Actually, even before I'd seen the shadow, I'd had quite an emotional day. It hadn't been easy, approaching the island that blustery summer afternoon, knowing that the place where I'd always been happy would never be the same again. As usual, half way over from Gleeport, the lurching, wind-whacked fishing boat had seemed to lose momentum. The engine didn't fail but, instead of making headway, the vessel seemed to stand still. It was the island that seemed to move, growing huge and detailed as it hurtled towards us in a whirl of white seabirds.

From where I sat in the bows of the *Spirit of Fife*, I could see the jumble of boulders at the foot of the greenstone cliff and the ribbon of pale gold sand where I'd played every summer I could remember. I could make out the concrete pier with its droopy skirt of seaweed and the slate-roofed cottage on the leeward slope. This had always been my most magic moment, when everything good lay ahead; fishing and swimming and picnics, tramping in the soft summer rain, listening to the counterpoint of the wind and the sea.

The difference now was that, although everywhere there was violent movement, there wasn't a whisper of sound. I could feel the wooden hull bucking like a giant rocking-horse, but I couldn't hear the slap of the waves. I felt the wind pouncing at my waterproof jerkin, but I couldn't hear its whistle and whoosh. I could see herring gulls swooping over the water but I couldn't hear their raucous, jubilant cries. I was a deaf kid with hearing aids that didn't work. The island fragmented through my self-pitying tears.

I was still snuffling and wiping my cheeks with my cuff when the *Spirit of Fife* drew alongside the pier. As her skipper, our friend Andy Macklin, lassoed an iron bollard and tied the boat up, Dad put his hands on my shoulders and turned me towards him. He didn't comment on my tear-stained face; the poor guy was used to it, God knows. Reluctantly I fixed my eyes on his bearded mouth, reading the exaggerated movements of his lips, teeth and tongue.

"Time to go, Nicholas." T-AY-M T-OO G-OW, N-I-K-OW-L-A-S. "Remember your rucksack." R-EE-M-E-M-BR –

Snarling with annoyance, I squirmed away from Dad's huge brown hands. It wasn't the lip-reading that narked me so much; I was a good learner and was quite chuffed that I'd cracked it so quickly. What I resented was having to concentrate while people said such damn stupid things. Any fool could see it was time to go and if I didn't pick up my rucksack I'd fall over the bloody thing. Scowling, I staggered with it to the gangplank, shrugging off Dad's hand as he tried to steady me. Instead of helping him and Andy to heave our luggage and boxes of provisions onto the pier, I squatted on the rucksack, shivering in the squally, unseasonable wind.

That was when I saw it. The sun had been scampering in and out of rainclouds since morning, but now a bright shaft pierced through, falling like a spotlight on the pier. Suddenly everything had a shadow, the *Spirit of Fife*, the luggage, Dad and Andy and I and – someone invisible. I could see the silhouette of a thin, bare-legged figure in a short skirt on the damp concrete – but nobody it could belong to.

More puzzled than scared, I called, "Dad! Look!" but he was too hard at work to heed me. Andy, who was doing us a favour, had to get back to Gleeport before the tide turned. As I gawped at the strange shadow, the sky clouded over and it disappeared.

At the time, I didn't pay much attention to the seagull perching on the bollard, fixing me with its cold, colourless eye. All seagulls have a baleful stare; there's nothing sinister about it. And, on an island said to take its name from the flocks that nest in every fold and cranny of its cliffs, there was no reason to suppose it was the same one perching on the gatepost when we arrived at the cottage – or on the outhouse roof when we went out before supper to stretch our legs.

I don't know how late it was before I fell asleep. There was an old grandfather clock in the kitchen downstairs that Dad always wound up as soon as we arrived; its tinny striking in the night used to annoy Mum and me till we got used to it again. Now it would have wakened the dead before it wakened me. What I do know is that, in the trance-like moment before I slid into sleep, I heard voices singing. Of course, I thought they were inside my head.

2

I Only Lived for Music

No matter how late I went to sleep, I'd always woken early. When I was small – in the days when we'd been a happy, normal family – I used to climb into Mum and Dad's bed and give them grief, wriggling and poking and chattering when they were still half zonked. Later on Mum had persuaded me – if "persuaded" is the right word – to stay in my own bed until I was called. I didn't mind, because by then I was old enough to read and study my scores and listen to music through my headphones.

Since my illness I'd got into the habit of just lying on my back, staring at the ceiling and going over in my mind all the hellish things that had happened to me. Mum, who had a genius for putting her foot in it, had once told me that I should try to put the past behind me and think of the future. TH-I-N-K O-V TH-I F-YOO-T-YOO-R. As if.

5

On the morning after I'd seen the shadow, I woke into a featureless world. Overnight fog had crept into the river mouth, rubbing out the moon and everything else in sight. The old-fashioned furniture in my bedroom had shape without detail and the window was a woolly grid on the drab grey wall. I knew Dad would eventually come to get me up.

"Eight o'clock, son. Breakfast's ready." AY-T O-K-L-O-K, S-U-N, B-R-E-K-F-A-S-TZ R-E-D-AY.

I'd gone to sleep with my mind full of the shadow, but habit's powerful. Rolling over, I went straight into my usual morning mode.

It's tragic to remember that, before something really appalling struck me, I'd thought being called Nicholas Moonlight was a tragedy. OK, so I looked cute in photographs with my floppy black hair and bright blue eyes, but I was really wet, skinny and small for my age and pampered by parents who'd never expected to have me. Over forty and twelve years married, the poor chumps couldn't believe their luck. According to Auntie Sadie, my christening was like a state banquet at Buckingham Palace.

I didn't go to nursery school. Because my mum was older, she didn't see the point. For my first four and a half years, she gave me all her time and a great deal more. Designer gear, designer teddy bears, paints, books, jigsaws, boxes of Lego – the Early Learning Centre must have made a fortune out of Mum. The only thing I wanted that I wasn't allowed to have was a dog, because it might moult on the carpet and poop on the lawn. Neither sulks nor charm offensives (and I was good at both) made any difference. Mum could be quite tough in those days.

Being so sheltered, I had no idea how bizarre my name was until the day I started school and Miss Marshall read it out from the class register: "Nicholas Danskin Moonlight." She blinked incredulously and puckered her thin mouth. Taking their cue from her, all the other kids laughed. Being four and wimpish, I burst into floods of tears.

To be fair, most of the kids stopped teasing me after a while. I suppose there were funnier things to watch than me red in the face and looking as if I'd swallowed a lemon. But there was one guy, Gerald Slade, who just couldn't let up. I was a moony loony, the cow jumped over me, I was made of green cheese. If ever there was a stupid moon joke to be made, big Gerald was sure to make it and, because they thought he was cool, the other kids were sure to snigger. I was jealous of everyone called Millar or Taylor or Grant.

Surprisingly, since I was so spoiled, I didn't get a lot of sympathy at home.

"Try to laugh it off," advised Mum. "Think what it's been like for me. I was Kitty Dumphy before I married Dad, so I've had two silly names to your one."

Dad, God help him, seemed chuffed to bits to be called Dr Simon Moonlight.

"It's an old Scots name," he informed me, just in case I thought it was Japanese. "We're descended from a brother

7

of Thomas Moonlight, who emigrated to America and became Governor of the State of Wyoming. Being called Moonlight didn't hold old Thomas back, did it?"

Maybe not, but old Thomas didn't have Gerald Slade in his class at primary school.

What Dad was too modest to say was that being called Moonlight hadn't held him back either. He was a marine biologist who taught at Edinburgh University and jetted around the world, advising governments on everything to do with the sea. At school he'd been clever and good-looking. He'd been cross-country champion and played rugby for Scottish Schools. I reckoned it had been easy for him to laugh off jokes about his name. Even if it hadn't, he'd had someone to share the pain. There was a guy in his class called Xavier Boastie.

In my class I had an enemy, Gerald Slade, and no close friend. I told myself it was because no one wanted to team up with a guy called Moonlight, but deep down I knew there were other reasons. Nobody likes a wee runty guy who can't take a joke. Nobody likes someone who persuades his mum to complain to the headmaster that her sunshine boy is being victimised. Then there was my music. Even if I'd been as cool as Harry Potter in every other way, my taste in music would have made me an outcast.

All the other kids in my class were rap and heavy metal freaks, and I just couldn't get my head round rap and heavy metal. They thought anyone who liked classical and played the violin was a total nerd. When I joined the choir at Holy

Trinity, you could have heard them laughing in Australia.

Which was sad, but what was I to do? I suppose I might have pretended, but I'd have had to suppress everything that mattered to me. I got along well enough in most subjects except PE, but I only lived for music. I started playing the piano when I was two and I had my first violin lessons at three and a half. In the evenings, when other kids were out on their bikes or aping rappers down at the youth club, I was playing Mozart's sonatas and hurrying to choir practice along the leafy pavements of Morningside.

> *"Hear my prayer,*
> *O God, incline thine ear . . . "*

It wasn't that I had much time for God. I liked Father Lochran, but to me his prayers and sermons were just boring interruptions of the music. What I liked was the clear sound of my own voice soaring into the dusty arches of the roof, and the feeling of power it gave me. Yet it was because Father Lochran thought that God had given me a gift that I got what should have been the opportunity of a lifetime.

"Nicholas, can you come round at five on Tuesday? I want to make a recording of your singing. I have a friend who teaches at St Augustine's Music School in Kent . . . "

I was in ecstasy – until an hour later I crashed into our kitchen and gasped out the good news to Mum. Then the shit really hit the fan.

"Absolutely not," she hollered, waving the iron like a

9

lethal weapon. "You're only eleven. You won't eat vegetables. You'd hate living away from home. I'd hate you living away from home. I don't approve of private education. I want you to grow up here in Edinburgh with me."

Needless to say, some bits of this rant were truer than others. Typically Dad, when he came home later in the evening, was more reasonable.

"You know Nicholas is gifted, Kitty, and St Augustine's really is the best. Let him make the recording with Father Lochran and we'll take it from there."

Mum didn't like it. She sniffed and scowled and I scowled back. But, two months later, she was the one who drove me south to Kent for an audition and an interview. When we came out of the Music School she was weeping like Niagara Falls and I was grinning like a Cheshire cat.

My singing and violin had won me a scholarship to St Augustine's and a place in the Cathedral choir. By September, when Gerald Slade and his cronies were settling into Primary Seven with Mr Angus "Hannibal Lecter" Hodge, I would be far away. For the next six years I'd be living and studying with people who shared my interests and would have better things to do than tease me about my silly name. I was going to have a fresh start. At last, I was going to make friends.

It was on Thursday 12 June, the day of the school sports, that I developed a splitting headache during the lunch break. My teacher, Miss Stevenson, was sceptical at first.

"Oh, come on, Nicholas. Just because you tripped in the egg-and-spoon race last year . . . "

Eventually she took me to lie down in the medical room and after the sports, when Mum would be back from work, she ran me home in her car. As I stumbled up the path, sweating and whimpering with pain, I saw a rash like a dusting of red pepper on my bare arms and hands.

3

No More Mr Nice Guy

Even now, I can hardly bear to remember what happened after that humid summer afternoon. I have a vague recollection of being rushed to the Royal Infirmary, choking and vomiting in the ambulance, but of the days that followed, when I was lying at death's door, I remember nothing.

It was only much later that I understood the horror of the meningitis outbreak of which I was the first victim; five pairs of parents keeping a round-the-clock vigil beside their kids; others queuing for vaccinations, appearing on television with terrified faces, demanding assurances the doctors couldn't give.

Three of my schoolmates were ill but recovered. A five-year-old boy died. What happened to me was something in between. When it seemed that all hope was lost, the doctors asked Mum and Dad's permission to give me an experimental drug. They were told that it would "in all probability damage my hearing", but just might save my life. Did my parents know that this was doctorspeak for "make me completely deaf"? I don't suppose they even thought about it. They did what any normal parents would do; they grabbed a pen and signed the consent form. I lived, if you could call what I was left with living.

I won't pretend that I behaved well. In fact, I behaved atrociously. As it dawned on me that I was trapped for ever in a silent world, I changed from a reasonably well-behaved kid into a snarling animal. Terrified by my loss, I screamed and swore and lashed out at Mum and Dad. When I wasn't exhausted – which I was a lot of the time – I tore up my books and trashed the sitting-room. Mum gave up her job at the library and Dad had to take time off work to help her control me. Late at night, when they were grey-faced with exhaustion themselves, I sobbed like a baby in their arms, repeating over and over, "I can't hear music. Why didn't you let me die?"

Mum wrote, "*Because we love you so much,*" on a piece of paper and held it up for me to read. Schmaltzy but no doubt true. In my watchful, bitter state, however, I couldn't help perceiving another truth about Mum and Dad.

Sure, they were grieved for me, but they were also grieved for themselves. Their normal, musically gifted child had been snatched away from them. All their hope for my future, their future as the parents of a promising young musician, had been snatched away too. In their fifties, they would have to cope with a disabled teenager. Right now, they had to cope with a regressive eleven-year-old having tantrums like a toddler, farting and peeing on the carpet to annoy them. No kidding, they'd have been better off with a dog. Their friends stopped coming to the house because I was so embarrassing. Anyone normal would have pitied them, but I wasn't normal. No more Mr Nice Guy.

Of course, Dad had to contact St Augustine's and say that I wouldn't be taking up my scholarship. Meanwhile I had to be educated and, when the first hellish weeks of rage and disbelief were past, I was hauled off to a hearing clinic. Actually it was a deafness clinic, just as a health centre is really an illness centre, otherwise why the hell would you be there?

While Mum and Dad sipped tea and looked like my grandparents, I sat in a cabinet with headphones on and a button to press when I could hear a sound. Score: zilch out of twenty, but they gave me hearing aids anyway. I thought they looked like glass earrings and I hated them.

A week later, I began to have lip-reading lessons with Miss Maxwell: "Watch my mouth very carefully, Nicholas." W-O-T-CH M-AY M-OW-TH V-E-R-AY K-AY-R-F-OO-L-AY, N-I-K-OW-L-A-S. I'd be watching mouths for the rest of my days.

At home, I could just stand Dad's pale, bearded lips but Mum's drove me ape. Miss Maxwell had told her to stop writing me notes so now, when she wanted to communicate, she stuck her chops right into mine. She had a big mouth with pink lipstick and gold whiskers at the corners of her upper lip. When I wasn't wiping spit off my face, I got familiar with every filling in her teeth.

"Look at me." L-OO-K A-T M-EE. "I'm speaking to you." AY-M S-P-EE-K-I-NG T-OO Y-OO.

Her anxiety did my head in. I came close to hating her.

In November, when leaves covered the garden paths like yellow satin and mist slipped along evening pavements, Mum's younger sister Auntie Sadie came to stay. Since by then I was on pills and comparatively tame, she took me back to Dundee while Mum and Dad went to Dublin for a break.

Auntie Sadie, who wasn't married, lived alone in a quiet street near the river. I'd always liked her because she was cool and let me have one of her cats in bed with me. She couldn't be bothered cooking so we always got supper from a takeaway in the Perth Road; fish and chips, haggis and chips, pie and chips, chicken and chips.

"Mum wouldn't approve of this," I remarked, as I tucked in.

"Then tell her we had lettuce," Auntie Sadie replied.

She also let me mess about in her studio, and that's what I did those cold, weepy November days. While Auntie Sadie worked on her book illustrations at a drawing-board by the window, I sat at a table and made a picture of Seagull Island.

First I drew the outline like a huge shoulder heaving up out of the water, with the cliff like a soldier's epaulette. I drew the cottage and the track winding up from the pier. I swished on a blue wash for the sky and dabbed on thick aquamarine for the sea. I spattered white for the gulls and spent ages trying to mix the tints of the island; pale gold for the sand, a dozen greens for the grass, amethyst for the shadows of afternoon.

"That's not bad," said Auntie Sadie, tipping my head up casually as she passed with a mug of coffee. She didn't bother pulling exaggerated faces and I understood her just as well. "The sky's a bit flat, though. Take a thicker brush . . . "

It was nice of her to want to help, but I was already losing interest in the picture. I quite liked art, but I knew I wasn't skilled enough to paint the things I loved most; the movement of the sea rinsing the shore, the sand like yellow jumbo cord at low tide, the spindrift reeling wildly above the rocks. I'm not sure why, before I discarded it, I took a felt pen and drew two tiny figures, one chasing the other along the beach. Sometimes I think my haunting must have started then, but I suppose it might just have been coincidence.

After Easter, wearing the hearing aids through which I could hear a distant sound like a pan being clattered with a metal spoon, I went back to school. Mum and Dad wanted me to stay in mainstream education, keeping up an appearance of normality in the face of a very different reality. I spent two hours every morning alone with Miss Maxwell and on Fridays a social worker came to see me.

"How are you getting on, Nicholas?"

"Fine, Mrs Sprott."

"Any problems you'd like to talk about?"

"No."

For the rest of the time I sat at the front of the class, staring at the red tongue and moist lips of "Hannibal Lecter" Hodge. I was the only person in the class not terrified by his roaring. Actually he was OK to me, and my classmates did their misguided best to be kind. The girls tried to lead me around as if I was blind. The boys lent me comics, and moon jokes were now off limits. Even Gerald Slade made an effort, offering me some yucky pot noodle on a plastic spoon.

I was too depressed to tell him where to put his pot noodle, though I could think of a number of places. In fact I was so depressed that Hannibal spoke to Mrs Sprott and she contacted Mum. Mum took me to our GP, Dr MacGrouther, who changed my pills so that I could be pepped up instead of calmed down.

Maybe the pills were to blame, or maybe I'd just got into the habit of being poisonous at home. During the next six weeks I cut up my bedroom curtains with scissors and stuck the lavatory seat to the pan with superglue. I made mud balls and threw them at Mum's knickers when they were hanging on the rotary-drier in the garden. I spread peanut butter on the piano keys and farted pungently in the sitting-room when Mrs Sprott was making a home visit. Every day Mum and Dad looked more like old-age pensioners.

Crisis point came on 15 June, my twelfth birthday. Last year I'd spent the day in a coma in the Royal Infirmary. This year Mum, keeping her sanity as well as she could, laid on all the treats she'd provided in happier years. There were heaps of streamers and a jazzy paper tablecloth, my favourite pasta and a birthday cake at tea time, presents heaped on the sofa for me to open afterwards.

When we sat down, I honestly didn't mean to wreck the party. There had been moments recently when I almost felt sorry for Mum and Dad. I managed to say, "Thanks, that was cool," when Mum took my plate away after the pasta. Even the birthday cake didn't rile me, though it was right over the top with twelve big candles and my name in bright blue icing. So it was a pity, when Dad had lit the candles and I was preparing to blow them out, that I glanced across the table at Mum. Mouthing widely in my direction, she was singing, "*Happy Birthday to You . . .* "

Talk about insensitive! It nearly blew my mind. I was lifting my fist to smash the cake when suddenly I had a better idea. Grabbing a candle, I set fire to the tablecloth. The streamers caught and my birthday tea went up like a towering inferno.

Just for a moment, I was stunned by what I'd done. Mum was flapping at the flames with a dish towel, making the blaze worse.

"Simon! Do something!" I saw her scream.

Dad snatched up the kettle and poured water all over the table, putting out not only the tablecloth and streamers but the remaining eleven candles as well. It was so ridiculous that I began to laugh hysterically. As Dad moved towards me, I ducked under his arm, bolted upstairs and slammed my bedroom door. My legs gave way suddenly and I sat on the floor for a long time.

At last, when I'd been to the loo and put on my pyjamas, a note was pushed under my door. It was the first I'd had since the lip-reading began, and knowing that my own mother couldn't face me actually made me feel guilty. Not for long, though.

"Nicholas, why are you behaving so badly? Can't you see? This is happening to us too."

Happening to them too? Like hell it was. Trembling with rage, I grabbed my saddest but still most precious possession and stumbled downstairs into the yard. In the still summer twilight, I smashed five thousand poundsworth of violin against the garage wall.

It was almost dark when Dad opened my bedroom door and padded over to me. Lifting me up from my tear-soaked pillow, he put his arms round me and held me close. I rested my aching head against his chest, taking comfort from his familiar, pepperminty smell. After a while he put me back and switched on my bedside lamp. Avoiding his unhappy, exhausted eyes, I concentrated on what he had to say.

"Nicholas, I have an idea. Why don't we go to the island for a few weeks, just you and me? Mum will go to Auntie Sadie and maybe join up with us later. We'll go fishing and watch the seals at Largo Point. What do you say?"

I said, "Yes," because just then anywhere away from Mum sounded close to paradise.

Three days later we landed on Seagull Island and I saw a shadow without a body on the pier.

4

Fog

Not long before my illness, sitting at our kitchen table, Auntie Sadie had offended us by remarking that she was spooked by Seagull Island.

"I don't know why you three like that eerie place so much. It gives me the creeps," she said.

We all stared in huffy astonishment. To us, Seagull Island was the least creepy place on earth. It wasn't like the isolated Hebrides, with nothing but the grey Atlantic between them and America. Seagull was an east-coast island, tucked comfortably into the estuary of the river Forth. From one side we could see the red-roofed fishing villages on the coast of Fife, from the other the cornfields of East Lothian. Fishermen and people on pleasure boats waved to us when we were on the beach and the cottage, owned by a colleague of Dad's at the University, had its

21

own generator, computer terminals and telephone lines. Creepy? Do me a favour.

"You're in a minority of one, Sadie," said Dad shortly, and it was true. All our other family and friends practically begged to share our summer holidays. If there wasn't room in the cottage, they brought tents. We had barbecues and made music in the kitchen as the sun went down.

But Auntie Sadie, with her green hair and cool earrings and funky velvet pinafores, was used to being in a minority of one. She looked at us calmly with her clear grey eyes.

"You're all so noisy, I don't suppose you notice," she said. "That island's like all deserted places that were once inhabited. In the silence, you can sense ghosts."

Mum and Dad were plainly embarrassed by this sort of talk.

"Another potato, Nicholas?" Mum asked stiffly, while Dad suddenly remembered a phone call he should have made.

I just thought Auntie Sadie was daft. Not until the first couple of days alone with Dad, trapped in silence and the thickest fog I could ever remember, did I begin to think about what she'd said.

Like Auntie Sadie, Dad on his own was an easy companion. He called me Nic, a name Mum disliked and didn't allow at home. He did tend to stick his face up close to mine, but since he only asked occasional questions like, "Do you want a mint?" or, "Beans or sweetcorn with your pork pie?" I wasn't too hacked off.

When Dad had got the generator in the outhouse going, he set up his computer and began to work. He was writing a book about marine gastropods, aka sea slugs, and was behind with it due to my meatball behaviour at home. I read sci-fi and messed about with my laptop. In the absence of Mum's pink lips and cute whiskers, I wasn't tempted to trash anything.

Unfortunately, as I wound down in one way I felt myself winding up in another. Maybe I was missing the usual summer stir of guys having fun. Certainly I was jittered by the persistence of the fog, breathing coldly round the cottage, slavering on the windows and reaching in whenever I opened the outside door. The memory of Auntie Sadie's words about ghosts began to scratch uncomfortably at my mind.

I hadn't been brought up to believe in the supernatural. I knew that, outside imagination, there was nothing weird about sea fog. I also knew it was just possible, as Dad had said, that the shadow had been "a trick of light". So why was I so sure it wasn't? And why was I so disturbed by the solitary seagull, just visible on the roof whenever I went out to fetch wood for the stove? Because the damn creature was always there. Even when I flapped my arms and chucked pebbles, it wouldn't go away.

By the third day, when Dad and I were both beginning to feel like prisoners, the fog thinned enough for us to climb the drenched, brackeny slope to the cliff top. The last two hundred metres were steep, and we were out of breath as we spread our waterproofs and sat down on the sandy summit.

"Want a mint?" aked Dad, producing two from his trouser pocket.

"Yeah, thanks," I replied.

We sat sucking the mints, peering down the guano-streaked columns to the crawling sea below. A watery sun was trying to shine. Through shifting vapour I could make out Inchaed, a weedy, barnacled islet attached to Seagull Island by a twenty-metre causeway. For a while at low tide it was accessible on foot, though crossing wasn't something I'd ever enjoyed. The causeway was narrow and slippery and, when the tide turned, the sea surged back with terrifying speed. Now the causeway was deeply submerged and the strange, conical rock that dominated the islet reared up like the neck of a great sea serpent.

I felt shivery and a heartbreaking thought came into my mind: *"This is a terrible place."*

Then – it happened again. I was on my feet and was waiting for Dad to get up when the sun sliced through the sky. A wet finger pointed down, touching Inchaed with faltering light. The shadow of the rock appeared on the lichened surface and, standing on top of it, I saw the shadow of a human being.

"Dad!" I screamed. "Look, down there! It's the shadow . . ."

Only it was too late. Dad was having trouble with the zip of his jerkin. By the time I'd got his attention, the shadow had disappeared.

5

Voices

"Nic!" I could see Dad doing his best to be patient. "You know it's impossible. You can't have a shadow without a body."

"I've seen it twice."

"Whatever you saw, it wasn't that."

Sitting across the table from Dad after supper, I could see fear magnified through his horn-rimmed glasses. No prizes for guessing what he was thinking: *God help me. First the guy goes deaf, then he goes off his trolley.* The minute I was in bed he'd be e-mailing Dr MacGrouther, fixing up for me to see a shrink, begging for stronger pills. *Watch my mouth. You've lost it, son.*

I'd been on the point of telling him about the seagull, but now I saw I'd been stupid to tell him anything. I'd already had some counselling, fixed up by Mrs Sprott, and

25

hadn't been impressed. The thought of a full-blown shrink made me back down without a fight.

"OK. You're right. Let's play Scrabble," I said.

The relief in Dad's eyes was pitiful but, as I opened the board and tipped the plastic letters onto the striped tablecloth, I couldn't help feeling he'd let me down. It wasn't good knowing that if something spooky really was happening on the island, I'd have to face it alone.

The fog had hung around well into the evening. Finally it dispersed in the time it takes to play a game of Scrabble. When I went upstairs, a cheesy green moon was climbing the violet sky. From my half-open window I could see the lights of the Fife coast, strung out like a necklace of golden stars. For the first time in my life, they seemed very far away.

On the first two nights on the island, I'd gone to sleep thinking I could hear singing. It hadn't bothered me a lot because it sometimes happened at home. The memory of music hadn't yet faded, and I reckoned it was an illusion caused by my deep longing to hear it again. What happened the third night was spectacularly different.

Although I'd felt tense since seeing the shadow in the afternoon, I was also completely bushed. I'd only been reading for a few minutes when my eyes felt itchy. I groped for the switch and went out with the light. I don't know which woke me, the bright-as-day moon shining on my face or the voices. Yes, voices, floating in through my window, as achingly clear as if I'd never gone deaf at all.

I sat up in bed, wide awake and totally amazed.

> *"Moon and stars, bless the Lord!*
> *Light and darkness, bless the Lord!*
> *Praise him and make his name*
> *great for ever!"*

Just then I was too happy to have room in my head for puzzlement, let alone fear. The soprano voice could have been my own, and the deeper voices backing it were as rich and confident as any in Father Lochran's choir. For a while I was content just to listen, but then something peculiar occurred to me. I'd never sung in Latin, because Father Lochran liked modern choral music sung in English. Yet I knew the singing outside was in Latin and, even more weirdly, I was translating it easily in my head.

> *"Benedicite maria et flumina Domino . . .*
> *. . . Seas and rivers, bless the Lord . . ."*

Mind-boggling, but did I care? Just then the music was so beautiful, my restored hearing so miraculous that all I wanted was to find the choir and join in.

Slipping out of bed, I threw open my door and leapt downstairs. Taking a deep breath, I unlatched the outside door and stepped into the chilly night. Then – nothing. There was no one in sight and the music was fading, as if the singers were sailing away from me over the moonstruck sea. Tears of disappointment welled in my eyes.

I was still standing in the yard when a thin light glimmered behind me. My own shadow quivered on the ground and, to my horror, another loomed at its side. When a hand was lightly laid on my shoulder, I got such a fright that I screamed. But it was only Dad, drawing me back into the kitchen, pushing his kind, anxious face into mine.

"Nic, I heard you coming down. Did you –"

I knew he was going to say, "Did you hear something?" but he checked himself in time. It wasn't a question I needed to ask him. Clearly he hadn't heard anything but my footsteps on the creaky stair. For a moment he squinted at me, his eyes sunken and short-sighted without his glasses. Then he made a typical grown-up's assumption.

"You must have been sleepwalking." S-L-EE-P- W-AW-K-I-NG. "I'll make you some hot chocolate, then you must get back to bed."

I could see from his expression that the idea of me sleepwalking bothered Dad, but there was no way I could put him right. He'd thought I'd gone barmy when I mentioned the shadow. It wasn't hard to imagine his pop-eyed look if I told him I'd heard a ghostly choir singing in Latin, which I'd understood.

I sat mutely in an armchair with a blanket wrapped round me, watching him pad around in his old grey dressing-gown, heating milk and pouring it into a mug. While I drank the chocolate, he boiled the kettle and refilled my hot-water bottle. He did all the other fatherly things, escorting me upstairs, giving me a hug and tucking my duvet round me.

"I'll leave the doors open. Call if you want me," he said.

Yet as he put out the light and returned to bed, I'd never felt so lonely in my life.

6

Shadow Play

In the morning, Dad brought me breakfast in bed, a sure sign that he thought I wasn't well. Since my illness he and Mum had watched me like hawks, fretting unnecessarily if I seemed tired or off-colour. Sometimes their concern irritated me, but I suppose it was comforting to know that, even if I'd wrecked everything for them, they preferred having me to facing life without me. Dad dumped a tray with buttered toast and a mug of tea across my knees and looked me over carefully.

"You look peaky," he mouthed. P-EE-K-AY. "Try to have another sleep."

I didn't bother pointing out that I always looked peaky; it was the shape of my face. When Dad had gone downstairs I drank the tea and ate the toast but I was too rattled to sleep again. When I'd finished I dumped the tray on the floor and pulled the duvet over my head.

To be honest, my first thought was that I wanted to get to hell out of this place. I'd already been spooked by a shadow and a beady-eyed seagull, and now there were ghostly singers to add to the loony list. Auntie Sadie had been right. Seagull Island was eerie and I had enough problems without that.

As I sucked toast crumbs out of my teeth, however, it occurred to me that I now had an extra problem – how to get off the island without being killed by Dad. We'd barely arrived, schlepping clothes, computers and tinned food to last a month. Unless I could give a credible reason for wanting to leave, he'd think I was just being bloody-minded again. Dad had a longer fuse than Mum, but even he must have a cracking-point.

Eventually I realised that, if I was determined to go, I only had two options. One: I could tell Dad the truth, that I was being haunted. Two: I could tell a mega porky and say I was having headaches again. Either way there would be a God-awful fuss; hospital visits, an appointment with a shrink or a brain scan, Mum barging back from Dundee before the shards of the violin had been emptied out of the wheelie-bin. I could see her mouth already. *"It's all right, darling. Mummy's here."* M-U-M-A-Y-Z H-EE-R. Oh, pur-leeze!

Maybe the thought of the horrors waiting at home made the prospect of staying put more attractive. But there was something else that perhaps only another deaf person could understand. As I lay with my eyes shut, the memory of the singing came surging back and I had an overpowering desire

31

to hear it again. Of course it was supernatural, but it hadn't been frightening – just amazing, bursting my silence with a glory of sound I'd thought was lost for ever. Of course it might have been a one-off but, if I ran away, I'd never know what might have been. I told myself that the shadow hadn't been frightening either, and as for that dorky seagull – well, it was just looking for food scraps, wasn't it?

As if to prove me right, a week of ordinary days went by. Although there was a stiff breeze that made you think twice before you took your fleece off, grey mornings cleared and sunshine glittered on the sea. Dad and I did the usual island things, fishing at the pier and collecting shells at low tide. We dabbled in rock pools, peered at jellyfish and brought home bladderwrack like black grapes on a string. For the first time in more than a year, I was chilling out. I barely thought about the shadow, and the seagull on the roof seemed more absurd than threatening. I ate well and Dad stopped giving me furtive, anxious looks.

The only spoiler, apart from the mega one of being deaf, was that I had to hang around so much on my own. Perhaps I was getting more reasonable, because I did try to be patient about Dad spending time on his book. But I still got cheesed off playing computer games and kicking a lonely ball around the yard.

"I wish Sandy and Angela were here," I said wistfully, meaning the cousins who usually shared my summer holidays.

"Gone to Spain," replied Dad shortly.

He was too kind to point out that my headbanging and farting in public had sent all our friends fleeing abroad on holiday, but I got the message.

It was while I was bored and feeling friendless that the supernatural again intruded into my life.

Although we'd had a week of sunny days, night mists had hidden the moon. On the evening when I next saw it rising like a squashed orange from the dark estuary, I thought of the voices and my chest tightened mysteriously. Before I got into bed, I made sure that my window was open and my bedroom door off the latch. I wasn't certain that, even if I heard music, I'd have the courage to go out again – but if I did, I'd be sure to go quietly this time.

I intended to stay awake until the moon came up the sky, but days in the fresh air made me sleepy and I soon dropped off. When I was shaken awake by music, my room was flooded with sulphurous light.

> *"Nights and days, bless the Lord!*
> *Praise him and make his name great*
> *for ever!"*

In fact, courage didn't enter into it. Spellbound by the voices I rose, tiptoed carefully down the edge of the stair and slipped out into the yard. This time the singing didn't fade away and I thought it was coming from the other side of the cottage. Breathless with expectation, I scooted round the corner. The choir was still invisible – but I saw the shadow. Thrown by the high, remote moon, it was stamped small and sharp on the whitewashed wall.

Why wasn't I scared out of my mind by something so flaky? Because I was hearing music. It was so magical that I'd no space in my head for fear. As I stood watching, the shadow moved, its thin legs paddling along the wall. It crooked its arm as if it was inviting me to follow. The voices chimed on as it slipped away across the grass and I scurried after it. I was actually giggling, as if I was larking about with a friend.

Jinking round the yard, hiding behind the outhouse, the shadow was teasing me. Whenever I got close it jumped away; I'd see it jigging on the roof or leaning its elbow against an upstairs windowsill.

"Not fair," I squealed, but the shadow just wiggled its fingers and danced away.

When it flitted down to the beach I went too, running in my bare feet through the looping skeins of the incoming tide. The water was freezing and I was only wearing pyjamas, but I hardly noticed the cold. I was quite a distance from the cottage when I realised that the voices were dying away. But the shadow was still weaving along, so I pelted after it to the place where the beach peters out among the rocks. When it froze suddenly I was running too fast to stop. I trod on it, as if it was a mat lying on the sand.

The singing cut out and a fierce jolt like electricity shot from my foot, twisting my whole body. Hugging myself in pain, my hands clutched unfamiliar material. To my horror, I realised that my cotton pyjamas were gone. I was wearing a tweedy, knee-length tunic with long, loose sleeves. I'm sure I was screaming as a stray cloud drifted across the moon.

7

A Day Out

"We're going over to Gleeport today," announced Dad unexpectedly, as I went into the kitchen next morning. "I need a haircut and so do you. Don't want you looking like Struwwelpeter, do we?" You get questions like this when you have elderly parents. If you don't know who Struwwelpeter was, don't ask. As I ate my cereal, I got the message that Andy was going to pick us up at half-past eight and another boat, the *Bluebell*, would bring us back on the evening tide. "We'll have lunch," Dad went on, "and go to St Andrews in the afternoon. S-AY-N-T A-N-D-R-OO-Z.

"Sounds cool," I nodded.

After my terrifying experience in the night, I reckoned a day away from Spook Island was exactly what I needed. I'd be able to chill out and, hopefully, start working out what the hell was going on.

Once on board the *Spirit of Fife*, however, I found it hard to shake off my perplexity and deep unease. While Dad chatted to Andy through the wheelhouse window, I sat watching the island withdraw across the rippling green water. I'd have given anything to dismiss last night's weird events as a dream, but I just couldn't. I had no idea how I'd got back to the cottage and upstairs without waking Dad, but I could remember crawling under my duvet, my teeth chattering with cold and thinking I'd never get warm again.

For most of the crossing my mind was bursting with questions. Who were these invisible singers a deaf boy could miraculously hear? Whose was the shadow and why, when I accidentally trod on it, had I seen my body dressed in clothes that weren't mine?

I had no answers but, as the cheerfully busy harbour and quaint pink and white houses of Gleeport zoomed towards me, I made some strong resolutions. I would never let anything so scary get to me again. If I heard the singers, I'd hide under the duvet until they went away. If I saw the shadow, I'd scarper. The seagull could go to hell and I would not, repeat not, be lured into any more silly games.

Talking myself up like this made me feel better. As I climbed the rusty ladder from the deck to the quay, I assured myself that I was in control. When I saw a seagull studying me coldly from the top of the harbour wall, I made a rude sign at it and stuck out my tongue.

Apart from one hiccup, Dad and I had a pleasant day. When we came out of the barber's we went to Boots for toothpaste and shampoo, then down to the harbour again to watch Andy's crew unloading the catch. After fish and chips at the Gleeport Hotel, Dad got our car from Andy's yard. In pleasant sunshine, we drove along the winding coast road.

A smoky haze softened the Bass Rock and North Berwick Law, but Seagull Island was abnormally clear, like an embroidered cushion behind a glass screen. I tried to look away from it across the fields, but I could only keep my eyes turned away for a few seconds. I had an alarming sense that the island was attracting me like a magnet. I was thankful when the road curved inland and it disappeared.

The busy, golf-crazy town of St Andrews gave me a welcome respite. Dad and I played a round of putting, guzzled ice cream and went to a bookshop. I stocked up on sci-fi and bought a paperback called *Islands of the Forth*. Dad, who was the world's greatest clutcher at straws, thought this was a sign that I was getting interested in normal things again.

"You must show that to Mum," he enthused, as the shop assistant slipped my purchases into a plastic carrier bag. "She knows a lot about the islands."

I didn't answer, partly because I didn't believe him and partly because I minded being mouthed at so obviously in a public place. Taking her cue from Dad, the shop assistant gave me a plump, sympathetic smile.

"Twenty-two pounds ninety-five, please," she said, stretching her mouth as if it was made of chewing-gum.

She was lucky I didn't break her glasses.

Since the *Bluebell* wasn't due to sail until nine o'clock, Dad suggested we should go to the cinema, then drive back to Gleeport for a bar supper. I only agreed because I was tired; you can take it from me that silent movies are seriously stale.

The *Bluebell* was late leaving harbour and it was well after ten o'clock when once again I approached Seagull Island. Dad, taking the opportunity of some normal conversation, was chatting to the skipper while I sat up in the bows. In spite of the tension I felt in returning to a haunted place, I couldn't help admiring the lavender sky and the white moon hanging like an oval lantern above the cliff. I was startled when my eye was drawn by a light at the far end of the beach. Suddenly my mouth went dry and I felt my nails digging sharply into the palms of my hands.

On the grassy bank above the spot where I'd stepped on the shadow, a small church had appeared. It had a cross at one end of its dark roof, grey stone walls and a lighted window in its gable, facing the sea.

While I stared with my mouth open, figures emerged from a door in the side of the building and began to file down a little path onto the beach. They were dressed in dark hooded garments that hid their faces. Each carried a candle that shone steadily in the gathering dusk. I knew they were monks, holy men who lived in communities and spent their lives praying to God. Miss Stevenson had told us about them in history lessons at school.

As the monks began to walk in single file along the shore, I saw at the end of the line two young boys in shorter tunics and with bare legs. While the *Bluebell* ploughed her soft furrow towards the pier, the familiar voices floated across the water:

> *"The heavens tell of God's glory:*
> *The sky shows the work of his hands . . . "*

The chanting was so loud and the scene so vivid, I was sure that the others on board must be aware of them too. I was shocked when I turned and saw Dad leaning on the side, laughing and gassing with the skipper and his mates.

"Oi!" I shouted, flapping my arms to attract their attention. I only turned my back for a moment, but just then the singing snapped off in the middle of a bar. When I looked again, the monks and their church had disappeared.

8

Aidan

Of course, I'd been a fool to imagine that I could lie in bed and do nothing while the monks were singing. However uncanny they were, I was a deaf musician and they were offering me what I wanted most in the world. Not that I got it immediately. For three days after I'd seen them on the shore, storms swept the island, wiping out the Fife coast, threatening to uproot the cottage and hurl it into the sea. I couldn't hear the howl of the wind or the impatient spatter of rain on the windows, but the thud and vibration made me want to scream.

While I huddled over the stove, trying vainly to concentrate on *Superman vs the Terminator*, I began to hunger for the singing as if I was dependent on a drug. When at last the waning moon poked its head above the horizon, all my resolutions had melted away. I didn't notice the irony of the words:

"Let dreams vanish
With the ghosts of darkness . . . "

and it didn't even bother me when I saw that the shadow had come indoors. When it touched down on the floor between the window and my bed, I got up and stroked it with my toe. I still felt a jolt, though it wasn't so painful this time. Once again a rough tunic clothed my body. As the walls of my room melted, I was out on the hillside in daylight. I could hear birds singing and the throaty sound of the sea.

I was standing on a sandy path a stone's throw from the church. Across the water I could see the coast of Fife, but its villages were gone and grey forest grew to the water's edge. Behind the church, sheltered by a fold in the hillside, I saw a settlement. There was a circle of small, turf-hatted stone huts surrounding two larger, rectangular ones. From a hole in the roof of the nearer, a twirl of smoke rose into the still, ice-blue sky.

Like the landscape, the season had changed. The roofs of the buildings were furry with white frost. I was poorly dressed for winter and my hands and feet tingled painfully. As I stood blowing into my fingers to warm them, I heard an impatient voice.

"Come on, Nic! If we don't hurry and fetch the water, Brother Ternan will be after us with his broom-handle."

Starting violently, I turned and saw a boy about my own age coming out of the nearer large hut. He was dressed as I was, in a grey tunic with a cord for a belt. Instead of socks he had strips of material wound round his feet and calves, held in place by the criss-cross lacings of his sandals, Glancing down, I saw that I had them too.

As he came towards me, the boy's thick red hair was a bright splash of colour on the pale landscape. His eyes were sea-grey and he had a wide, happy mouth. He was carrying two leather buckets with rope handles, one of which he pushed at me.

"Move," he said.

"Right," I replied.

A rough dry-stone wall enclosed the settlement. Curiously I followed the boy through a gap and up onto the hill. The frost was melting fast and before long my feet were wet as well as cold. Quite soon we reached a place where there was a spring, like a watery mouth in a beard of withered bracken. A gutter had been carved from rock to channel the water, and I could hear it bubbling and splashing into a stone tank below.

Imitating my companion, I swung my bucket into the tank and began to stagger back with it, getting my tunic soaked as I went. But the discomfort was nothing compared with the amazement of sound; the swoosh of breaking waves, the seagulls' screaming "Kee-ya, kee-ow," the slap of my own feet on the earth. I was almost crying with joy.

That's not to say I didn't find it weird – but now something happened even weirder than the red-haired boy calling me Nic. He was stronger than I was and, as my arm began to ache, I couldn't keep up with him.

"Hold on, Aidan," I called peevishly. "You're going too fast for me. I'm spilling the water."

At the sound of his name, the boy put down his bucket and waited for me to catch up.

"Sorry, Nic," he said kindly. "Brother Ternan said to hurry because he wants to get the bread made before midday prayer. Come on. I'll help you with the bucket."

Carrying his own in one hand and supporting mine with the other, he led me between the little huts. I knew these were called "cells", perhaps from school history, though I'm not sure now. When we walked through the door of the large hut, it was like walking into a furnace. The sudden blast of heat made my head reel.

As my eyes adjusted to the windowless light, I saw a room with blackened walls. A fire glowed on a stone slab in the middle of the hard-earth floor and smoke hung below the roof like a drab blanket. At one end of the room there was a shelf with wooden plates and bowls. At the other was a table where a dark, greasy young man stood with his wide sleeves rolled up to the elbows. He was gutting fish with a knife, throwing the heads and entrails into another bucket.

"Take over here, Aidan," he said abruptly. "Little brother, come and help me knead the bread."

It was just as well I hadn't been told to gut fish. That was Dad's job in our house. It was easier to follow the monk as he mixed water with grey flour and melted fat, and help him to shape handfuls into round, flat cakes. By the time we'd transferred them to the stone by the fire, I was sweating like a pig.

"Wash your hands, little brother," said Brother Ternan, pointing to an iron bowl on the table. "It's nearly time for prayer."

"Yes, brother," I heard myself reply.

While I was drying my hands on my tunic, a bell rang out. Instantly Brother Ternan and Aidan pulled up their hoods and hurried out of the kitchen. As I followed, the shock of the winter air made me shiver like a leaf.

I saw monks emerging from their cells and from the other large hut. With their hands tucked into their sleeves, they glided towards the church. I entered last, after Aidan. The interior was gloomy and I smelt a scent like honey rising from two tall candles on a little stone altar.

The monks – eight of them – stood in two rows facing each other. I stood opposite Aidan. Glancing round, I saw faces young and old, eyes blue and grey and brown, all looking at me. Without prompting, I took a deep breath and began to sing:

> *"I will give thanks to God;*
> *His praise shall always*
> *be in my mouth . . . "*

The music was simple, an unaccompanied line of melody without any of the rich variations I was used to. But I sustained it, the deeper voices of the monks providing a wall of sound against which I could bounce mine like a silver ball.

> "*I will give thanks to you, Lord.*
> *I will sing praise to you.*"

My voice was as wonderful as ever. I was ecstatic.

"You weren't singing," I whispered to Aidan's back as I walked at the tail of the procession from the church to the kitchen. I was surprised when he turned, sniggered and gave me a good-humoured push.

"Abbot Ninian says I'm not to sing," he told me. "He says God will be better pleased if I just move my lips. Anyway," he added teasingly, "you make enough noise for both of us. Just as well I'm going to be the lord and you're going to be the monk, eh?"

Now here was something strange. I hadn't a clue who this guy was or what he was talking about. But I swear I felt a pang of jealousy so intense that, just for a moment, I hated him. Before I could reply, the monk in front of us turned his head and glared.

"Shut up, pests," he hissed angrily.

My envy faded as he turned away and Aidan cheerfully thumbed his nose.

If I said that the rest of the day passed in a dream, I'd fail to convey how real it felt. I sat on a stool in the kitchen, eating roasted fish and the oatcake we'd made earlier, while an old monk called Brother Oswald read aloud to us from the book of Psalms. I had a drink of water from a shared wooden cup and left the kitchen still hungry. I helped Aidan to feed hens and wipe round the kitchen, and played with him on the beach when our work was done.

Whenever a procession formed, I fell in behind Aidan. Though it suited me because I usually didn't know what to do, I was narked that he was always in front of me. He couldn't even sing, while I was the star of the choir. Still, he was cheerful and friendly, whereas the older monks seemed stiff and remote.

As the early winter dusk rubbed out the sea, I again poured out my voice in the draughty church. After we'd asked God to protect us from the terrors of the night, each monk lit a small candle from the tall ones on the altar. Still singing, they filed out solemnly. As I stepped out, I looked up and saw a dark, soupy moon stroking the edge of the hill. Suddenly I thought of Dad and, without knowing why, I blew out my candle.

9

Letters in the Sand

"Can you amuse yourself for a while, Nic?" asked Dad the following afternoon. "I've got to send some e-mails."

"No sweat," I replied agreeably, and saw him blink in surprise. I suppose a reasonable me was hard to believe in, after all I'd put him through. "I'll go for a walk along the beach," I added.

"Don't do anything dangerous," warned Dad, sounding like Mum.

Raising two scornful fingers to the seagull on the outhouse roof, I sloped through the yard and down onto the sand. Actually, it was a relief to be on my own. I was keen to look for traces of the monastery and equally keen not to be pestered with adult questions.

"What exactly are you looking for, Nic?"

Don't ask.

Needless to say, when I'd woken in the morning, I'd been tempted to believe that my visit to the monastery had been a dream – except that it hadn't been dreamlike and it was hardly the first wacky experience I'd had. Besides, I could remember exactly how, after blowing out the candle, I'd returned to the here-and-now. I hadn't been in bed, but standing in a pool of moonlight in the middle of my room. I'd been there when Dad came upstairs and saw me through my half-open door.

"Everything OK, Nic?"

"Yeah, fine."

"Go to sleep then, son. It's after midnight."

He'd confirm it if I asked him, but I didn't have to. In the absence of Mum and her Hoover, my bedroom was seriously uncleaned. When I'd opened my eyes in the morning, I'd seen the prints of my own bare feet on the dusty floor.

By afternoon, when I was tramping along the line of brittle seaweed and mussel shells thrown up by the tide, one thing seemed clear. If I really had spent several hours on the island in a time centuries ago, that time didn't follow the rules of now. I must have gone into the past and returned from it at the same moment. You'd think such a monstrous notion would have blown my head, but it didn't. Maybe I was just arrogant, stupidly chuffed because I'd made it there and back again. But I think it's more likely that already something strange was happening to my mind.

I was sure I knew exactly where the church had been, just above the spot where I'd first touched the shadow –

Aidan's shadow, obviously, since he was the only monk who wore a short tunic and had long thin legs. When I got to the place I scrambled up eagerly onto the grassy bank above the beach. Standing on site, I looked around me – and was disappointed. There wasn't a single stone sticking up from the turf. The church and the other buildings had vanished without trace. I couldn't find the well where I'd gone with Aidan either and, to add to my vexation, spits of rain quickly became a downpour.

I'd stumped back to the edge of the bank and was pulling up the hood of my jerkin when suddenly I noticed something. Exactly where I'd stood on the shadow, flush with the beach and half obscured by drifting sand, there was a stone. It was dark grey, about half a metre square. Suddenly psyched up, I leapt down and ran over to it. When I'd scooped away the sand, I saw letters faintly carved:

EACA MONACHU

and underneath a sign like a cross with a diagonal line drawn through it. I hadn't a clue what these words meant but, as I traced them with my fingers, a dreadful sense of foreboding and despair crept over me. Starting back as if I'd touched a snake, I reeled home blindly in the pelting rain. My heart was still pounding when I was safe in the kitchen with my hands folded round a mug of hot tea.

"I'll need another hour, son, if that's OK," said Dad.

"Sure. I'll read for a while," I agreed.

I was glad enough to curl up in an armchair with a book, but too perplexed to concentrate. How, I wondered, could I have played all these summers on the beach without noticing such an unusual stone? It was obviously ancient, yet I'd never even heard it mentioned. It wasn't till Dad was getting supper ready that I remembered the book I'd bought in St Andrews, *Islands of the Forth*. Thinking it might be helpful, I fetched it from my room.

Unfortunately, from my point of view, the book was a swizz. It was really a tourist guide, concentrating on the large islands like Inchcolm and the Isle of May. Seagull Island only rated a couple of paragraphs near the end. I knew most of the stuff already; that the island was home to a colony of grey seals, that the last of a long line of lighthouses had been replaced by a lightship and demolished in 1989. It did say that a small community of monks had existed on Seagull in the eighth century, but nothing about buildings or a strange stone. Not much for £4.99, but there you go.

I was closing the book when Dad, who was waiting for the chicken casserole to heat through, wandered over to see what I was reading. When I looked up, I saw a troubled, yearning expression in his blue eyes.

"Nic, if you're interested, why don't you talk to Mum?" he said earnestly. "She studied the islands at university. She'd love to share what she knows with you."

The way he looked at me hurt me sometimes, and I'd have liked to please him. But I just wasn't in the mood to talk to Mum. I knew she'd gone to Auntie Sadie's to have a rest from me. OK, so I was having a rest from her too. But I still wanted information.

"When I was on the beach," I said, "I saw a stone with letters carved on it. Do you know anything about it?"

Dad looked completely blank.

"No, I've never seen it," he said. "But look – the rain has stopped. Why don't we take a walk after supper? Then you can show it to me."

Remembering my earlier fright, I felt reluctant to look at the stone again, even with Dad. But my curiosity was strong and, in the moist evening, I trudged beside him along the shore. As we approached the rocks I felt a shiver of apprehension, but I needn't have. We spent ages trampling and kicking the sand but the stone, like the monastery, had completely disappeared.

10

Brothers

I don't know if the weather that summer really was the worst ever, or if clear skies just mattered more to me. The next two nights were moonless and I slept badly, dreaming about St Augustine's and the choir at Holy Trinity. Starting awake, I lay tossing restlessly as tatters of music floated elusively through my memory. By the third day I was again like an addict gagging for a fix.

Dad took me fishing and we had out first shivery swim of the summer. The *Spirit of Fife* called in, bringing a parcel of games and new books from Mum and Auntie Sadie, but nothing lightened my mood. Unable to concentrate, I began to do silly things, like putting the teapot in the fridge and wearing my shoes on the wrong feet. I could see Dad watching me, worrying again about my "peaky" face.

"Feeling OK, son?"

"Yip."

All he'd said about the disappearing stone was, "Never mind. I expect the sand has drifted over it again," but I bet he thought I'd imagined the whole thing.

As well as the terrible hunger for singing, I began to long for younger company. I remembered red-haired Aidan and how cool it had been messing about with him on the beach. When at last the moon shone and I saw the shadow in the yard, I dropped the wood I was carrying and leapt onto it with both feet. Instantly I felt a warm glow on my face and heard the splosh of the waves.

To my surprise, I wasn't in the monastery but at Largo Point, a flat, rocky promontory on the island's northern shore. In lukewarm sunshine I was sitting on the glassy rock, dabbling my feet in a shallow pool. I was wearing my tunic and beside me was a leather bucket with fish in it and a jumble of fishing lines.

A little fire was burning nearby and Aidan, on his knees and with a smut on his pointed nose, was cooking a sprat on the end of a stick. As I sniffed the fragrant scents of the wood smoke and roasting fish, I had a moment of deep happiness.

"More wood, Nic," said Aidan. I reached for some dry driftwood and edged over to the fire. The fuel crackled sharply as I put it on. "Have you got the bread?" Aidan inquired.

Strangely, I knew where the bread was. Scrambling back to the cliff foot, I found a cloth bag containing some of

Brother Ternan's oatcake and four apples, yellow and wizened like old skin. There was also a thick glass bottle, its neck stuffed with straw to stop the water running out.

"These apples are horrible," I complained, dumping the provisions beside the fire.

Aidan glanced up at me through the shimmer of heat.

"Don't be grumpy, Nic," he pleaded gently. "We're lucky to have apples at all in May. Brother Ternan's pleased how well they've lasted through the winter."

While he went on cooking, I again dabbled my feet. If this was May, I thought, more than a few days had passed since I came visiting in the frost. Had no one missed me? And why were we here, instead of helping Brother Ternan and singing – in my case – in the choir? Aidan had shared out the oatcake and passed me a chunk of hot fish on a stick before I got an answer.

"It's good of Abbot Ninian to give us a whole day's holiday, isn't it? I suppose he feels sorry for us because we'll never share another one."

The trouble was that every answer suggested another question. I didn't want to say, "Why not?" because obviously I was supposed to know. I picked bones from a scrap of fish, then said tentatively, "Never?"

I saw a half-exasperated, half-pitying expression in Aidan's eyes.

"You know it's never," he said. "It's only a few weeks till I leave the island to join Earl Cathro's household. I've learned all the Latin I need here and now it's time for me to train to be a warrior. How else can I serve my king and defend my lands when I inherit them from Father?"

Although there was nothing boastful in his tone, I seethed with resentment. Who did this carroty prat think he was, swanking about *his* king and *his* lands? I could feel my lips puckering into the pout that used to drive Miss Stevenson ape. I knew I was spoiling a special occasion for Aidan, but I didn't care.

"What about me?" I demanded truculently.

Aidan's pleasant face hardened suddenly.

"You'll be a monk, little brother," he growled.

To my dismay, I began to howl like a baby that had lost its rattle. At once Aidan looked remorseful.

"I'm sorry, Nic," he said. "I know it doesn't seem fair, but I didn't ask to be born first. And it's father's decision that you're to be a monk, not mine. He does care about you – he's paid the church well to look after you. Besides, let's face it – you're not cut out to be a soldier."

I reckoned this was an insult, but I was too gobsmacked to challenge it. Did this guy really think I was his brother? I was opening my mouth to put him right when something chilling occurred to me. If I wasn't his brother, why was I behaving as if I was?

The question was so scary that I shied away from it like a pony frightened by a flash of light. I managed to stop blubbering but my happiness was gone. Aidan's too, from the sober look on his face. We cleared up in silence, throwing to the birds food that now tasted sour. After we'd had a drink, Aidan poured the rest of the water on the embers of the fire. I watched mumpishly as he put the bottle in the bag and tied it to his cord belt. Catching my eye, he smiled ruefully.

"Come on, Nic. Cheer up," he coaxed. "Still friends?"

"I suppose so," I said tightly.

"Then let's paddle and gather mussels," said Aidan, picking up the bucket. "The brothers deserve a treat too to celebrate our birthday."

"Your birthday," I corrected.

"Our birthday."

That was how I discovered that Aidan didn't only think I was his brother. He thought I was his twin.

That night, after I'd led the choir at evening prayer in the church, I went to bed at the monastery. The day had ended peacefully with me singing,

> *"How good and pleasant it is*
> *For brothers to live in harmony,"*

and Aidan grinning in the candlelight. Brother Ternan had been delighted with our bucket of bright blue mussels.

"We'll have them stewed with rock parsley for dinner tomorrow," he'd promised, his solemn young face much improved by a smile.

Aidan had thanked the chief monk, Abbot Ninian, for giving us a holiday.

"We had a wonderful day, Father. Our time together is so precious now. *Deo gratias*. Thanks to God."

The old man had blessed us, his blue-veined hand lingering longer on Aidan's head than it did on mine.

"Twelve years old! You won't be children much longer," he said with a sigh.

I had carried my candle from the church, three paces behind my twin brother Aidan, whom I loved and hated – but what was I saying? *He was not my twin brother*. As I wriggled into my tiny cell, feeling icy draughts slicing through its dry-stone walls, I reminded myself that I was Nicholas Danskin Moonlight, of 14 Thornybank Terrace, Edinburgh. *I was only here for the music*. Still wearing my tunic, I crawled onto a sack filled with damp straw and pulled up a grotty woollen blanket. Concentrating hard, I whispered, "Home," and blew my candle out.

11

A Strange Lighthouse

I don't suppose it will surprise anyone that, the instant I landed in the yard with my feet splayed where they'd touched the shadow, panic seized me. Scrabbling wildly to pick up the firewood, I rushed into the kitchen and slammed the door. Dropping the wood, I fumbled for the bolts that Dad never bothered to draw – as if locking the door could make the least difference to what was happening to me.

It won't surprise anyone either that, as I got into bed an hour later, I was swearing yet again that I'd had enough. I hadn't enjoyed the picnic and I didn't fancy kipping in my clothes on a damp sack. The notion that Aidan thought I was his twin brother was creepy. It was stupid to act a part in a play I didn't understand and whose ending I didn't know. I vowed that I'd hide under the duvet when the moon shone, etc, etc, etc.

And it won't surprise anyone that, by next morning, I was seeing things differently. Surely, I thought, as I lay in the grey dawn, I was worrying needlessly? It wasn't as if I didn't know how to get in and out of the "other world" where I could sing and hear perfectly. To go in, I touched Aidan's shadow. To come back, I thought of being home with Dad and blew out my candle. Since lighting candles was part of the monks' nightly routine, I would always be able to get back.

How secure that made me feel! Even when, almost immediately, the craving for music and Aidan's company again began to gnaw at my mind, I really thought I could choose and have control.

That day the sun burned away the mist quickly, and by breakfast time the sky was as blue and white as a willow pattern plate.

"Let's go fishing," said Dad, so we took our lines down to the pier.

I was on my knees, baiting my hook when the shadow came for me. When I saw it lying on the warm concrete I was surprised, which was silly because I'd first seen it right here, cast by the sun. Not that it mattered; as soon as it appeared, my hand jerked out and touched it – without the coaxing of music and in front of my father. So much for choice and control.

"Nic!" Aidan's voice seemed a long way off. "You're to come at once. The barge has arrived with the wood. Abbot

Ninian says if we all help we can get it unloaded and into the cave before morning prayer."

Struggling out of sleep, I forced open heavy, reluctant eyes. I was curled up like a slowworm on my damp bed, with Aidan crouching over me. Through the doorway of my cell I glimpsed the colourless island dawn.

"Push off," I said irritably, scrabbling for my blanket.

Mercilessly Aidan stripped it away.

"Up, Weasel," he said amiably.

Muttering and tripping over the loose laces of my sandals, I staggered after him across the dew-laden grass. Others were hurrying in their gliding, monkish way down the path to the beach. We tagged on behind them.

It was the first time I'd been down on the shore in monastery time and I couldn't help being interested. In place of the familiar concrete pier I saw a wooden jetty supported on tree-trunk legs. Alongside lay a flat-bottomed barge, low in the water because of its heavy load of cut logs and bundles of brushwood. I looked at it in perplexity. Such an amount of wood would have fed Brother Ternan's kitchen fire for two years.

"What's it for?" I asked – my first indiscreet question.

Aidan rolled his eyes and wearily tapped his forehead.

"Wake up, muttonhead," he groaned. "It's for the light, of course. Now tie your sandals and give us a hand."

Just then, not for the first time, something odd happened in my mind. As I knelt to tie my laces, it occurred to me that I knew what Aidan was talking about. On the other side of the island there was an islet. On it was a thin black rock, about three metres high. Bolted to its point there was an iron basket. On nights of evil weather, the monks lit a fire in it to warn mariners of submerged rocks. How silly of me to have forgotten.

As I stood up, I heard a rumble of wheels. Out of the mist came a high-sided cart, pulled and pushed by the monks. Two bearded bargemen, dressed in brown tunics and leggings, were heaving logs ashore. While the monks and Aidan, supervised by Abbot Ninian, began stacking them on the cart, I stood shivering in the drizzle. I wasn't strong enough to manhandle logs, I thought with a twinge of self-pity.

When the cart was full, Abbot Ninian thanked the bargemen and returned to the monastery. Four monks got between the shafts. With two pushing behind, they began to drag the cart along a gravelly path, past the grassy spot where one day our cottage would stand. Aidan turned to me, his red, sweaty face darkened by a scowl.

"What a lazy little rat you are, Nic," he said contemptuously. "Just because you can sing, you think you never have to get your hands dirty. Come and help with the brushwood, if you think you can bear the weight."

I was so furious I'd have punched his nose, if I hadn't been afraid of getting a harder punch in return. Sullenly I allowed Aidan to tie a huge, scratchy bundle of twigs to my back. When he and Brother Ternan had done the same for each other, we plodded after the cart. To add to my misery, the drizzle thickened to rain.

It seemed to take ages to get to the other side of the island, although unburdened you could walk the distance in less than twenty minutes. Eventually we reached a deep cave, where the monks were already busy unloading the cart.

As Aidan and Brother Ternan hurried to help, I stood staring down at the bleak islet. The tide was licking greedily at its slimy shore and the tall rock, with its spiky basket, looked like a rearing snake wearing a crown. I shuddered as I visualised the scene on a stormswept night, the fire flaring defiantly above the rampant waves. I'd seen the islet before, of course, but for some reason I couldn't remember its name.

"Come on, Weasel. All the work's done. Time for you to show off in church."

Startled, I turned to see Aidan's jeering face and the smirks of the monks. Leaving the empty cart at the mouth of the cave, they began to tramp back to the monastery. They didn't chatter, but there was a companionship among them that included Aidan but excluded me. As I trailed after them, my bitterness against Aidan was like puke in my throat. He had called me a weasel and a rat. I wouldn't forget or forgive.

Even when Abbot Ninian rang the bell and the dark figures began to hurry towards the church, my mood remained black. That morning, for the first time ever, I sang without love and joy. I didn't suppose anyone had even noticed, but someone had.

"Nic!" Aidan appeared while I was searching for eggs in the hens' nests along the wall. "Nic, I'm sorry. You didn't enjoy singing this morning and it was my fault. I forget sometimes that you're not as strong as me. I was the rat, not you."

It was a handsome apology, but I wasn't entirely satisfied.

"You also called me a weasel," I pointed out with a sniff.

Aidan gave a soft snort of laughter.

"You can blame Father for that," he said obscurely. "Anyway, we mustn't waste time quarrelling. Forgive me?"

How could I refuse? He never said anything mean without regretting it. He was the kind of friend I'd longed for all my friendless life.

"Of course," I agreed.

"Good." Aidan's teeth showed in a wide smile. "Let's do our chores, then we'll get spades and build a fort on the sand."

12

Another Nic

On that occasion I stayed at the monastery for several days, putting out my candle each night without a thought of leaving. It wasn't what you'd call a holiday, what with early rising and stingy helpings of monotonous food – fish, oatcake and sloppy porridge. There were also horrendous creepy-crawlies.

"What the hell are these?" I demanded one morning, shaking out my blanket on the wet grass.

Aidan peered closely.

"The black ones are fleas and the grey ones are lice," he informed me matter-of-factly. "You're lucky if you've never had them before."

"I've sure got them now," I groaned, lifting my tunic to scratch my behind.

Actually, I should have been less surprised. I'd already

noticed that the monks weren't heavily into hygiene. They never bathed and never changed their clothes. If they needed to pee they went behind the wall and if they needed more that that they squatted in the sand. Toilet paper, forget it. Mum would have passed out cold.

So why was I enjoying myself so much? Because I had the use of my ears. I could hear myself and others singing and hold normal conversations.

"Aidan, let's play a game."

"Yes. Noughts and crosses?"

"We don't have any paper."

"Who needs paper? All we need is two sticks and some wet sand."

It was fun having someone to hang out with, and it was worth any amount of discomfort to hear sheep bleating and gulls crying in the wind.

Not that we were always playing games. The business of the community was work. A lot of the time Aidan and I helped Brother Ternan, wiping plates, grinding meal and churning butter until our arms ached. In the morning we watched the elderly Brother Oswald milk his two brown cows, then we carried pails of warm, frothy milk from the cowshed to the kitchen.

In the evening we helped the shepherd, yellow-haired Brother Coelman, to bring the sheep and lambs from the hill to the shelter of the fold. This was my favourite job; the sheep were scatty and I thought the lambs were really cool with their cream fleeces and delicate ears.

For an hour each day, Aidan and I had Latin lessons with Abbot Ninian. Aidan wasn't much of a student, but I went on amazing myself with how much I knew.

"*Laborare est orare*. To work is to pray. *Cantate Domino canticum novum*. Sing to the Lord a new song."

The old monk called me Neacal. He pronounced it "Nicol", which I reckoned he thought was closer to Nicholas and more formal than Nic.

I was there when the monks went back to the islet at low tide to fetch the cart. I saw Brother Coelman climb a rickety ladder to fill the iron basket with brushwood and logs.

"Always best to be prepared," he said placidly.

It was a bright day and the sea was as unthreatening as a sheet of rippled glass. Yet it wasn't hard to imagine how it would be out here on a night of storm, with rain lashing and a gale whipping the legs of a poor monk struggling up the ladder to kindle the flame. It was too horrifying to think about and I was glad when we headed back to the shelter of the monastery.

Actually, the kind of life the monks led didn't appeal to me much. It was hard graft in a comfortless environment and even the younger ones suffered from rheumatism and toothache. Not being from a churchy family, I often wondered why they put up with it. It was only occasionally, when I glimpsed the rapture in their eyes as they sang and prayed, that I got a sense of what made them tick.

"O God, I long for you.
Like a dry, worn-out and waterless land,
My soul is thirsty for you."

The monks believed in God so intensely that they cared more for him than for the wives, children and possessions they'd given up to serve him.

Not that it mattered to me. I thought singing was a performance art, and being at the monastery just seemed a cool way to escape the tedium of life with Dad at the cottage. It was good knowing I could get back to him whenever I liked – and with no questions asked.

Which sounds neat, but there was a downside as well. I had moments when the sheer uncanniness of what was happening frightened me, and there were puzzles I couldn't solve. It was spooky that everyone at the monastery thought they knew me, spookier still that Aidan thought I was his twin. But spookiest of all was that sometimes I thought I was his twin. For hours at a time I forgot that I was Nic Moonlight, born towards the end of the twentieth century, and actually believed that I was another Nic, born more than twelve hundred years before. Flaky? And some.

During these periods my feelings about Aidan changed. On one side I was dependent on him emotionally and dreaded the day when he would leave the island. On the other, jealousy of his good fortune, which I'd already felt fleetingly, bit deeply into my mind. I could hardly bear the thought that, just because he'd been born half an hour before me, he was destined to be a wealthy lord and I a complete nobody. In two years, I realised desolately, my beautiful voice would break and I'd have no musical instrument to make the loss tolerable. I'd spend the rest of my life as a grungy monk, croaking psalms to an unjust God in whom I only half believed.

Envy didn't improve me. I began to take pleasure in anything bad that happened to Aidan. When he accidentally knocked over a pail of milk and Brother Ternan clonked him with the broom-handle, I laughed secretly. When he fell on the rocks and gashed his knee, I pretended to be sorry but I really wished he'd broken his leg. I was miffed because the monks obviously liked him better than me. "Little brother" wasn't a pet name, just a cold reminder of what was to come.

"Little brother, don't stand there dreaming! Wipe up this mess or you'll feel my stick!"

"Aidan, you've found some gulls' eggs. God bless you, my son."

I wanted to smash the eggs in Aidan's face.

These were shocking feelings and, when I snapped back into Nic Moonlight, I disowned them. Aidan was a nice guy, I reminded myself, and what the other Nic thought wasn't my business. All the same, by the end of a week, the odd behaviour of my mind was getting to me. One chilly morning, after an uncomfortable, itchy night, I decided I'd had enough. That night after prayer I'd blow out my candle and go home.

Before that could happen, however, something crucial and deeply unpleasant occurred.

"Aidan! Little brother!" Aidan and I were in the "writing-room", the large hut where monks spent hours making copies of the Bible with pens and coloured ink. We were practising lettering on scraps of parchment when Brother Ternan poked his greasy head round the door. "Your parents – Earl Robert and his lady – they're coming ashore," he gasped.

With a howl of delight, Aidan sprang to his feet and shot through the door. I put my own lack of enthusiasm down to the fact that I was entirely Nic Moonlight just then – but I was curious, all the same. Laying down my pen, I sauntered past the kitchen towards the church. Standing at the corner in the afternoon sunshine, I squinted down at the shore.

A large, brightly painted boat, manned by six oarsmen, was slipping towards the jetty. In its stern sat a black-bearded, youngish man in a long blue tunic with heavily embroidered sleeves. Beside him was a thin, pale woman in a purple cloak, with plaits of heavy, copper-coloured hair. As the man sprang onto the jetty and helped his wife ashore, Aidan rushed up to them.

"Mother! Father!" His voice was shrill with delight. "I didn't expect you yet. What a wonderful surprise!"

They were as pleased as he was. I watched them hugging him and affectionately tousling his hair.

"Aidan! How are you, lad?"

"My dear boy! How you've grown!"

I had a sudden, piercing memory of arriving home from summer music camp, of rushing up the path and throwing myself at Mum and Dad.

"Nicholas, we've missed you dreadfully!"

"Oh, Mum, I'm so glad to be home. What's for tea?"

The recollection faded as I lost hold of my own identity and slipped smoothly into the mind of the other Nic.

"Hey, Nic!" Aidan struggled free from the playfully wrestling arms of his father and grinned up at me. "Come on down! Mother and Father want to see you too."

Believe that, I thought bitterly, and you'd believe anything. As I slouched reluctantly down to the jetty, I could feel vibes of hostility jabbing the air. I was shivering, as if a sudden frost had blighted the golden afternoon.

"Well, Weasel, how are you?"

Weasel! How I hated that cruel nickname! I was too upset to reply, not that it mattered to my father. He stood grinning sneerily with his arm round Aidan. My mother examined me as if I was a slug that had crawled from under a stone.

"You smell of fish, Neacal. Oh well, I expect you'd like to kiss me. Come and get it over."

Frankly, I'd rather have kissed a crocodile, but I was afraid of being thumped by my father if I insulted her. As she bent down and held back her gleaming hair, I shuffled forward and made a snuffling noise some distance from her cheek. She couldn't have recoiled more sharply if I really

71

had been a weasel. Tears of humiliation flowed from my eyes.

"For God's sake, boy! Will you never stop snivelling?"

The scorching heat of my father's anger was so alarming that I turned and ran from the jetty. Stumbling and slithering through the dry sand, I reached a small cave scooped from the turf bank by the wind. Sobbing bitterly, I crawled inside.

13

Alarming News

The sun had gone round the side of the island and I was getting very cold when Aidan appeared suddenly at the mouth of the cave.

"It's all right, Nic," he said. "You can stop hiding. Mother and Father have gone away."

Since I was still in the mind of the other Nic, I was overwhelmed with relief. Alone in the cave, I'd been terrified that our father and mother would take Aidan away with them, and that I'd never see him again. As soon as I knew that hadn't happened, resentment against the affectionate threesome swept back over me.

"Push off," I snapped, but Aidan paid no attention. Crawling into the cave, he put a consoling arm round my shoulders.

"I'm so sorry, Nic," he said. "That was a really horrible visit."

"Not for you," I pointed out, shrugging off his arm. I was

taken aback when Aidan sniffed loudly and I realised he'd been crying too. "I suppose you thought they'd come to fetch you," I added bleakly.

Aidan gulped and wiped his nose on his sleeve.

"I suppose I hoped," he admitted, "though I'd no reason. I've always known I'd be here till midsummer. I just didn't expect to be told I'd have to stay even longer."

My spirits rose, but I was damned if I'd let him see I was pleased.

"Will you?" I asked coolly. "Why is that?"

Aidan's eyes brimmed with tears. Although he'd often comforted me when I was unhappy, I felt no pity for him. Leaning against the dry wall of the cave, I waited for him to go on.

"Father and Mother came to tell me about a change of plan," he said tightly. "I'm not to join Earl Cathro next month after all."

"Why not?"

"Because Earl Cathro lives in Caithness," Aidan said. "Norsemen have been raiding his lands, stealing his cattle and taking his people away as slaves. Mother's afraid I'll be in danger living with him. Father's going to look for another lord who'll take me on, but that may take a couple of months. Until then –" he bared his teeth in frustration "– I'm stuck in this hell-hole."

I was genuinely astonished.

"I thought you liked it here," I said. "You're always so bloody cheerful."

Aidan kicked a piece of driftwood petulantly into the sand.

"I haven't hated it," he said grudgingly. "I had to be educated somewhere, and the monks have always been kind." Then, without regard for my feelings, he let the truth come tumbling out. "But I'm not cut out to be a monk any more than you are to be a soldier. Monks live on islands to avoid company, but I like people, Nic. I want to meet girls and have fun with other young folk. I want to learn to ride and use a sword and have fine clothes to wear." He caught my eye and added defensively, "You can't grudge me. I've looked after you for twelve years and – well, let's face it. I'm not like you."

"In what way?" I inquired icily.

"In what way?" I heard Aidan's voice squeaking with incredulity. Worse, as he turned towards me, I caught in his eyes a chilling glimpse of the distaste his parents had shown. "Oh, don't ask," he groaned.

> *"Do not be afraid of danger by night*
> *or of sudden attacks by day,*
> *For God shall send his angels*
> *to protect you*
> *and keep you safe wherever you go,"*

I chanted in the glimmering candlelight. We sang these words of comfort every night, but they had never sounded more empty – and not only because of the emptiness in my own heart. Before the service, in the most peaceful twilight imaginable, Abbot Ninian had gathered us all on the grass outside the church.

"My sons," he said gravely, "you know that Earl Robert and his lady honoured us with a visit this afternoon. I'm sorry to say that the earl brought bad news. Since spring the fierce men of Norway have been attacking our northern coasts, burning villages and killing innocent people. Monasteries have been looted, their monks murdered and their treasures carried away."

A shiver seemed to pass from one monk to another. They were too disciplined to cry out, but they stared at Abbot Ninian with round, frightened eyes. Wearily he tried to reassure them.

"Earl Robert thinks we are probably safe meantime. There's plenty of plunder up north and, since the Norsemen return home in winter, it may be many months before they come near our coast. Even then, because our island is upriver and we have nothing to steal, they may pass us by." Seeing that "mays" and "probablys" weren't convincing his audience, Abbot Ninian raised his voice impatiently. "Come now, brothers! Do you suppose, if Earl Robert believed attack was imminent, he would leave the young lord Aidan in our care?"

To be fair to Aidan, he blushed scarlet at this crass question. It would have needed more that embarrassment, however, to cool my sense of outrage. The lord Aidan was to stay on the island only till his father found him somewhere safe to live. By the time the Norsemen turned their attention to the southlands, he would be far away, living in some swanky castle, flirting with girls and wearing fancy clothes. It didn't matter that his twin brother would be left behind, safe only if the Norsemen didn't think him worth murdering. Scowling blackly, I heard Abbot Ninian's final words.

"Earl Robert has warned me that we must do nothing to draw attention to ourselves. The light to help seafarers must remain dark while danger threatens us. We shall stay on this sheltered side of the island and pray to God to deliver us."

"Amen," mumbled the unhappy monks.

Whichever Nic I had been, it would have been hard to imagine a more hellish day. I could hardly wait to blow out my candle and get out of it. And this time, I swore, I would not be coming back.

14

In Two Minds

As if! As if an addict could face down addiction just by
flicking his fingers. As if by swearing not to return, I could
shake off the enchantment that now trapped me like a fly
in a pot of glue. I had barely landed back on the pier beside
Dad, the bait and hook still in my hands, when I realised
something ominous. So far, the past of the island had been
somewhere I visited. Now it began to visit me.

I'd always thought of ghosts as grey, ectoplasmic things
that could walk through closed doors and float above the
ground. Maybe I'd watched too many silly films on TV. The
figures haunting me now weren't like that; they almost
blinded me with colour. Whatever I was doing – eating my
breakfast, digging for sandworms, making up a jigsaw puzzle –
I saw them staring at me.

There was contemptuous Earl Robert in his gentian

tunic, standing by the sideboard with his arm round orange-haired Aidan. The haughty lady, with her auburn plaits and purple cloak, was sitting in a chair by the stove. Even the drab monks disturbed me with colour. I saw Brother Ternan's fiery face staring at me through the kitchen window and glimpsed Brother Coelman's buttercup head at the top of the stair. I opened the door and there, on the step, was a grey-faced Abbot Ninian, his sapphire eyes two piercing points of light.

There was no hiding place. My nights were ugly with dreams. Sometimes I was being attacked by an outsize seagull, trying hopelessly to defend myself from its wicked beak and tearing claws. Sometimes I was plunging from the cliff into the oily black sea. Most often it was the basket of fire on Inchaed that flared through my nightmares. A beacon of hope turned to a signal for disaster, it exploded into the night sky, blotting out the stars. I dreamt that I was slithering along the causeway with a leather bucket in my hand and a bundle of brushwood tied to my back. The tide was running in, sloshing cold water up to my knees, but I had to go on. If I didn't climb the rock and put out the fire the Norsemen, cruel Vikings with battle-axes and swords, would come and kill my mum and dad.

While these appalling images were stabbing my eyes, something even scarier was happening in my mind. Like a hand easing itself comfortably into a glove, the other Nic's consciousness was insinuating itself into mine.

I thought that instead of being born in Dundee where my

granny Dumphy lived, I had been born in a thatched hut inside a high wooden palisade. As I lay in my tiny straw-stuffed crib, I could hear leaves rustling and the gurgle of a stream at the bottom of a steep glen. Further off, I could hear wolves howling and I cried with fear. My nurse, a burly young woman called Fenn, had a grim sense of humour.

"There, there, don't cry. It's not wolves we have to fear in this house. We have your father . . . "

As I grew older, I knew that my name, Neacal mac Robert, meant "Neacal, son of Robert". The place where I lived was the fortress of my father, who was a powerful nobleman. There were many huts inside the fence, occupied by servants, guards, boy soldiers, huntsmen and dogs.

Brought up by Fenn, I scarcely knew my parents. My father didn't notice me unless he tripped over me. He called me "Weasel" and I learned to fear his foot in my ribs. My mother was beautiful but uncaring, more interested in her reflection in a bronze mirror than in mothering me.

Fortunately I had a twin brother, Aidan, whom I loved with all my heart. Although we'd been born together, he was bigger, stronger and more confident than me. Aidan was the one with bright ideas:

"Let's make a swing, Nic. I'll get some rope from the stable." I couldn't have made a swing to save my life. I watched while Aidan made it, gasping with admiration as he tied it to an overhanging branch and launched himself over the yawning lips of the glen. "Look at me, Nic! I'm flying . . . "

When I was persuaded to have a go, I fell off and skinned my knees.

"Let's trap a squirrel and keep it as a pet." Even for Aidan this was a challenge, but eventually he constructed a cage and baited it with hazelnuts. Only the minute a greedy red squirrel actually ventured in, Aidan was stricken by its heartbroken cries. "Oh, poor thing! How could I be so cruel? Open the trap, Nic, and let it go."

So I did, and wasn't in the least surprised when the angry squirrel chose my finger to bite. But I admired Aidan far too much to reproach him – and besides, I needed his protection. All around me were enemies; sneering servants, snarling dogs, arrogant bully-boys sent by their lordly fathers to be trained in warfare by mine. To them I was a joke. Their cruel jibes when they heard me singing hurt me deeply.

"What's that gruesome noise?"

"Yes, I hear it too. Don't tell me! Someone's bought a cat."

Aidan wouldn't stand for it.

"Leave Neacal alone, you mean pigs. Why shouldn't he sing if he wants to? It isn't his fault he can't do anything else . . . "

It was an opinion evidently shared by our father. On our eighth birthday, Aidan and I were summoned to hear Earl Robert's plans for our future. Aidan marched smartly into the round hall with its rows of gleaming shields and spears.

"You sent for me, Father. Have you something exciting lined up for me?"

I hung back in the doorway, snotty and dying for a pee. Mother was sitting upright on a stool with an embroidery frame in her lap. Black-haired Father straddled the hearthstone, turning a bronze cup in his long brown hands.

"Time for school, eh, boys?" he grinned. "Next week you'll both travel to the island where my old friend Ninian has a monastery. You, Weasel –" his windburnt face fleered at me in the firelight "– will study to be a monk. See you work hard, since I've had to pay in advance for you and it's all the living you'll ever have. You, Aidan –" he smiled dotingly at my brother "– will learn to read and write and be obedient before you start your real education as a warrior. We must make a brave, well-educated man of you, for all I have will one day be yours."

"Oh, thank you, Father!"

Aidan was almost bursting with happiness. While his mother kissed him and his father clapped him proudly on the shoulder, I skulked tearfully in the shadows. How could anything so unfair be happening? Wasn't I Aidan's twin? That was the moment when anger and jealousy began to poison my love.

In the dark cottage, isolated by my deafness, I struggled desperately to keep hold of my own identity. *"I am Nicholas Danskin Moonlight. I live at 14 Thornybank Terrace, Morningside, Edinburgh. My dad is a marine biologist and my mum is a librarian."* It was ironic, when you think about it. After years of complaining about the name "Moonlight", Nicholas

Moonlight was now the only person I wanted to be. Yet even as I repeated the words, I knew I was losing the battle. As the colours of the ghostly world burned ever brighter, my world as Nicholas Moonlight faded to a filmy grey, with only the seagull standing out like a splash of white paint on a dingy wall. Even Dad, hunched over his computer in the kitchen, looked as ghostly as I felt.

I've wondered sometimes why Dad didn't notice how zombie-like I'd become. God knows, he wasn't neglectful generally. I dare say he was just absorbed in his work and grateful, after a year of me headbanging, for peace at last.

Sometimes I was tempted to shatter his peace, freaking and screaming that I hated the island, I was spooked out of my head and I wanted to go home. I no longer cared about the fuss there would be; it might be the lesser of two evils. What stopped me was the chilling perception that it would make no difference. If I went home, the other Nic would come with me. It wasn't the island that was haunted, it was me.

I'd been back in the cottage for several overcast days when the sick desire for music again overwhelmed me. When at last the moon shone and I saw the familiar silhouette on my bedroom wall, not even dread of the Norsemen restrained me. Stretching out my hand, I touched it gently, like a brother.

15

Play Time

Perversely, when I returned to the monastery, Nic Moonlight seemed to be back in control. I could recall every detail of the other Nic's shocking early history. I was still raw with anger when I remembered the day when he'd been humiliated by his parents and terrified by the prospect of being murdered by Norsemen. Just for the moment, however, I was an observer rather than the occupant of his mind.

As I looked around me, I realised that time had moved on since my last visit. The freshness of early summer had become a little worn and stained. The grass was yellowing and the pink flowers of thrift had faded to grey tissue. Across the water in Fife, the forest roof was a darker, dustier green. But the perfect weather held with pearly mornings, golden days and violet twilights that lasted almost till dawn.

"God, I hate this island," groused Aidan, who wasn't the happy lad he used to be. "Sometimes I think I'll die here. You'd think Father could've got a place for me by now."

"Why doesn't he train you as a warrior himself?" I asked innocently.

"Don't be stupid," said Aidan irritably. "Whoever heard of a warrior being trained by his own father?"

I had no reply. I thought Aidan's eagerness to leave me was tactless but at least, as Nic Moonlight, I didn't have to cope with the other Nic's conflicting resentment and dread of separation. In fact, I'd have found these summer days quite relaxed, except that fear of marauding Vikings had run like a virus through the community. The monks started at shadows, and the longships with their dragon prows were never far from their minds.

"They ask God to protect them," observed Aidan, "but they don't believe he will. So why do they bother?"

This was a deep question that I couldn't answer, but I saw the point. If God didn't protect people who had given up everything to serve him, I couldn't expect much from him either. As a precaution I began to carry a stump of candle in the small leather bag that hung from my belt, although God alone knows how I thought I was going to light it.

The only thing that brightened the atmosphere, at least for me, was that Aidan, the monastery pet, had decided to rebel. As time passed and his frustration deepened, he relieved the tedium by playing practical jokes. One morning he came to church with a large rat hidden in his tunic. As I sang solemnly, *"I am fearful in my heart, Lord,"* he let it loose on the floor.

What followed was wicked. The monks couldn't have thrown bigger wobblies if the rat had been an elephant. They all flapped and jigged and the response, *"I am fearful and trembling; a horrible dread has overcome me,"* was accompanied by squeals of "Eek!" and "Shoo!" Terrified by the commotion, the rat ran up Brother Oswald's skirt and bit his knee. Abbot Ninian was absolutely livid.

"If this is how you behave when you see a rat," he thundered, "how will you behave if you see something really dangerous?"

Aidan got a mega ticking-off, but it didn't stop him. The next night he put a slowworm in Brother Ternan's bed. As the creature uncoiled coldly against his bare feet, Brother Ternan let out such a scream you could have heard it in Norway. This time Abbot Ninian sentenced Aidan to three days on bread and water, but the young lord was defiant.

"It's past midsummer. I'm not a pupil here any more. I'm a guest."

"Then try to behave like one," snapped Abbot Ninian.

You could tell, though, that the monks found it hard to be angry with Aidan. They had enjoyed having such an easy, good-humoured young person living with them. Maybe I was the only one who knew, from my own experience, that it's no sweat being good-humoured when you're getting everything your own way.

All the same, when Aidan was in a good mood I had cool times with him. Father Ninian had warned the monks to stay on the sheltered side of the island, but Aidan reckoned he was no longer bound by monastery rules.

"And you're not either," he assured me. "You can't be a proper monk until you're fourteen. So let's have some fun while we can."

I didn't think Father Ninian would see the distinction between a trainee and a proper monk, but what the hell. I was Nic Moonlight and I was only here for the music.

"Let's go," I said.

There were no more whole-day holidays, but Abbot Ninian had always been decent about giving us play time. In the hours when the monks were praying alone in their cells, we slipped away into the bracken. On the seaward side of the island, we swam and watched the seals sunning themselves on the rocks. We picked the dusty-blue bilberries that grew in the heather and ate them as we scanned the shimmering, empty horizon.

"I'll miss you, Nic."

"You know you won't."

"I shan't forget you, anyway."

One afternoon we returned home by the cliff path. Below us lay the barnacled islet with its primitive lighthouse, now forbidden territory to the community. But the fire was all ready to be lit next time and I could see the ladder wedged under the tall black rock. Even on a summer day the place gave me the creeps, but I was also fascinated by it.

"You'd think rain would put the fire out," I remarked to Aidan, as we rested at the mouth of the cave where the wood was stored. "Not to mention waves on a stormy night."

"Brother Coelman explained to me," Aidan replied. "If a storm's brewing, Abbot Ninian sends three monks to the islet at low tide. One gets a bottle of oil from the cave, climbs up the ladder and pours oil over the wood. Another gets a small fire going and prepares a torch tipped with oil-soaked rags. The basket's so high and the fire's so fierce, it's hardly ever gone out."

"What does the third monk do?"

"He brings more wood from the cave to feed the fire, and they all stay on duty until low tide next morning." Aidan sighed regretfully and added, "I used to beg Abbot Ninian to let me go on light-duty because it would be so exciting. Nothing doing, though – he said it was far too dangerous for children."

I had a terrible vision of frail figures clinging to the rock in a screaming storm, a mini-volcano dropping red-hot ash on their unprotected heads.

"You wonder why they do it," I said glumly.

Aidan laughed shortly.

"They do it," he said, "because good monks believe that God rewards kind deeds in heaven. That's why you'll never be a good monk, Nic." I knew the other Nic too well to protest but, before I said anything, Aidan couldn't resist another dig. "Even so, once the Norsemen are gone and you're a proper monk, I bet you'll have plenty of opportunities to go up the ladder and show how brave you are."

There were times, even as Nic Moonlight, when I'd cheerfully have pushed Aidan's face into a plate of porridge. What I didn't know, that sunlit afternoon, was that my days at the monastery as Nic Moonlight were almost over. A puzzle that had bugged me from the beginning was about to be horribly and dramatically solved.

16

A Face in Water

It happened after midday prayer, when the community gathered in the kitchen for dinner, the only proper meal of the day. Up till then things had been going well for me. I'd fed some fluffy new chickens, had my Latin lesson and messed about with Aidan on the sun-warmed sand. After prayer, Abbot Ninian had stopped me at the church door.

"You sang beautifully today, Neacal. I don't think we'll ever have another boy monk whose singing gives us such joy. Thanks to God for your wonderful voice."

One thing Abbot Ninian had in common with Father Lochran at Holy Trinity was that they were always thanking God when, in my opinion, they should have been thanking me. Still, a performer likes to be appreciated. When I sat down to eat my small ration of egg, bread and cheese, I had absolutely no reason to suspect that everything was about to go pear-shaped.

The usual drill after dinner was that the monks adjourned to their cells for several hours of Bible reading and private prayer. Today, however, Abbot Ninian had something else on his mind.

"You're all going to have your hair cut," he announced, casting a disapproving glance around the table. "I've never seen such a raggle-taggle bunch in my life." Abbot Ninian was nothing like as twitchy about the Norsemen as the other monks, but these days he was more peppery about trifles. "Fetch the scissors, Brother Ronan," he ordered.

There was no denying that the monks were a manky lot, as thin as sticks and with skin hardened by malnutrition and exposure to the weather. Not only were they unwashed but also horribly hairy, with bushy manes and long, tangled beards. Since there were no mirrors in the monastery, none of us ever saw our own faces but, as Abbot Ninian spoke, the monks glanced furtively at each other. Blushing, they ran their fingers through their own beards and hair.

"Yes, Father," they chorused in their childlike way.

I'd had my hair cut short the day I went to Gleeport with Dad. I was surprised when Abbot Ninian lined me up with the rest, but I knew better than to argue. When Brother Ronan, a dark young monk with blackcurrant eyes, had fetched a clumsy pair of iron scissors from the kitchen cupboard, I waited my turn in the queue.

Actually, it was quite good fun watching the monks

being barbered. It didn't take long, since Brother Ronan wasn't what you'd call a stylist. Each monk had barely time to ease his behind onto a stool when the scissors went snip-snap and hanks of hair, grey, brown or gold, tumbled to the ground. It was a bit like seeing sheep being shorn, go-in-woolly, come-out-shaved, with the same expression of bald surprise as the monks reeled away into the sunshine. Brother Ternan stood by with his broom, looking pained as he swept hair off his already grotty kitchen floor.

I was giggling at Aidan, clipped like a skinhead, when Brother Ronan called out, "Next please!" As I jumped onto the stool, I heard him guffaw. "This one won't take long," he said.

What happened then was absolutely horrible.

I had always had soft but very thick black hair. Sometimes I wore it spiked with gel, but more often I just let it flop about my ears. It was my best feature, I reckoned in the days before disaster snuffed out my interest in the way I looked. The instant I felt Brother Ronan's cold scissors at the nape of my neck, I knew something was wrong. My head shouldn't feel like this.

A loathsome feeling crept over my scalp and my shoulders tensed apprehensively. I heard a few feeble snips then, sick with anxiety, I glanced down. On my tunic lay a few miserable wisps of rust-coloured hair. As Brother Ronan blew sharply over my shoulder, I saw them wafting pathetically onto the floor.

That was the moment when, dry-mouthed with horror, I

understood. The reason the monks recognised me, the reason Aidan thought I was his twin brother, was that I didn't look like me. It wasn't only the other Nic's mind I had, it was his body. And what did he look like, this boy with skimpy ginger hair? As I recalled the revulsion I'd seen in the eyes of Earl Robert and his wife and even, momentarily, in Aidan's, I could scarcely repress a scream.

Leaping from the stool, I ducked past Brother Ternan and dived out into the open air. Panting with terror, I pelted away from the monastery, past the church, past the wooden jetty, along the sandy path. On the cliff-bound side of the island, I dropped down onto the shore. The tide had gone out, leaving pools among the rocks. On trembling legs I lurched about until I found one that was glassy and deep. Sinking onto my knees, I clenched my teeth and looked.

Yes, I was Aidan's twin, all right. The resemblance was almost as horrifying as the difference. Besides red hair, we had the strange similarity that close relations can have, even when no two features are exactly alike. But Aidan's hair was thick and shiny; the little I had was dandruffy and as dry as dead grass. His grey eyes were wide and candid; mine were small and dull, blinking foxily through short white lashes. His cheeks were rosy, his lips full and generous; my chinless face was pinched, my thin mouth puckered at one corner into a permanent, involuntary sneer.

I was like a goblin, a grotesque caricature of my twin. You would have thought that, at our birth, a fairy godmother had given every gift of beauty, health and good fortune to him, and none to me – apart from my voice, that cruelly temporary gift.

Writhing with fury and self-disgust, I threw up all over the rock.

17

Beauty and the Beast

When I was a little boy, Mum and Dad used to read me bed-time stories. My favourites were the ones where some hideous person was really good and caring inside, like the fearful monster in *Beauty and the Beast*. It was cool when the beast turned into a handsome prince, because you felt such a nice guy really deserved a break. You have to be older to suss that in real life even nice guys can forget that kind of miracle.

The problem with Neacal mac Robert was that, by the time he was twelve, what you saw on the outside was a perfect match with what was inside. He looked what he was, a dissatisfied, malicious imp. OK, you might feel sorry for him. Nature hadn't been kind to him, and naturally his brother's good looks were galling. Anyone normal would be shocked by the unfair and cruel way he'd been treated. But

95

nothing alters the fact that, by the time he got his claws into me, Neacal was a seriously twisted individual.

At the beginning, I thought I'd been drawn back in time by music, restored to me by some magical but benevolent power. Too late I realised that my weakness had been exploited by a malign person who wanted to take over my mind. What's more, he was succeeding. As my personality as Nic Moonlight faded, I forgot my parents, my home and my whole former life. I became Neacal mac Robert, the goblin whose face I had seen in the pool. I thought his shabby thoughts and concentrated on achieving his petty, sick desires.

Once I was Neacal, I was, in my mad way, realistic. Because I was powerless to harm my father and mother directly, I found an easier target in Aidan, the only person who had been loyal and kind to me. My affection for him waned as I raked through the ashes of our relationship, turning slights into grievances, brotherly spats into bitter quarrels.

Although I knew that, in a family like ours, the first-born son always inherited his father's title and wealth, I convinced myself that Aidan had schemed to rob me of my share. Because my face didn't fit, he and my father had conspired to dump me in a monastery and leave me to rot. While I played with Aidan on the sand, I swore to give him a leaving present he'd never forget.

Of course I was too crafty and self-protective to do anything spectacular too soon. I had a plan I knew would discredit

Aidan in the eyes of Abbot Ninian and, more importantly, his father. I must take care, however, that no blame fell on me. First I would spend some time building up my brother's new reputation as a mischief maker.

It was a doddle getting Aidan into trouble, after the incidents with the rat and the slowworm. During the week following the hideous revelation at the pool, I put a dead mouse in the milk pail and scattered sheep droppings on the church floor. I popped a live crab into Brother Ternan's hood and a sand eel into my own.

"Father!" I screamed, rushing into the kitchen while the monks were settling down to dinner. "Someone's put a squirmy thing in my hood!" It was good to see every eye focus on Aidan as Brother Coelman tweaked out the eel and held it up between finger and thumb.

Next I shuffled the pages of the Bible Brother Ronan was copying and left his desk in a shambles. I put sandworms in the butterchurn and upset an inkpot, spilling the precious ink on the floor. The monks were bewildered; between terror of the Norsemen and hurt at the heartless behaviour of a boy they loved, their peace had been completely destroyed. Abbot Ninian was furious.

"Aidan, did you do these stupid things?"

"I must have done, Father."

"Then spend your free time today and tomorrow on your knees in the church. Ask God to forgive you, for you're disappointing us all."

I could see this rebuke hurting Aidan, but he wouldn't

betray me. Not until the evening when I opened the gate of the sheepfold and let the sheep run away onto the hill did his patience snap.

"You're a mean little runt, Nic," he snarled, pinning me against the kitchen wall. "You don't know the difference between a joke and an outrage. Suppose the sheep had run over the cliff in the dark and been killed? I never thought I'd say this, but I'll be glad to be rid of you. If you do one more rotten thing, I'll tell Abbot Ninian the truth." His face was scarlet and his hands were itching to thump me, but Aidan could never sustain anger. As I began to wail, he backed down. "Sorry, sorry. I didn't mean it. I know you're unhappy. Please don't cry."

I was glad he felt bad and I wanted him to feel worse.

"Aidan, I am unhappy," I sobbed. "I don't want to stay here without you. Take me with you. I could be your servant or something."

This was over the top. Squinting through my tears, I caught the conflict of horror and amusement in Aidan's grey eyes. I knew exactly what he was thinking: *What? Me turn up at a lord's gate with this ugly dwarf snuffling at my heels? "Hello, I'm Aidan mac Robert and this creep's my servant." Like hell.* What he said was less vehement, but almost as brutal.

"Come off it, Nic. You know that couldn't happen. Father would never allow it. Anyway –" the impatient shrug of his shoulders told me how boring this subject had become "– you've got to get used to it. We've had good times, but now we have to part. End of story."

If he thought that, he underestimated me. That was his weakness; he didn't have enough imagination to suspect the effect his matter-of-factness had on me. I was just poor runty Nic, a burden he'd be glad to shed. But, because he'd been kind in our childhood, he still believed that in the end I'd wish him well. I squeezed out some more tears.

"So you don't care if I'm murdered by Norsemen?" I whimpered.

Aidan groaned.

"Don't be stupid. Of course I care, but there's nothing I can do about it. I may be murdered by Norsemen myself."

But not without a sword in your hand, you cold-blooded bastard.

The beginning of the end came suddenly, on a cool, autumnal morning. Aidan and I had finished our stint at the cowshed and, while waiting for the bell to ring for prayer, we'd gone down to the jetty. We were lying on our stomachs, idly dropping pebbles into the clear green water, when a boat emerged from the mist. Aidan was on his feet in an instant.

"Look, Nic! Someone's coming," he cried. "I wonder if it's Father?"

Aidan could think of nothing now but the coming of his father. Even this mellow, extended summer couldn't last for ever, and he was dreading having to spend another winter on the island.

"It isn't Father," I said flatly, as the small, unadorned boat bobbed closer to shore. "He wouldn't be seen dead in a tub like that."

"A messenger, then," guessed Aidan, determinedly optimistic. As the boat came alongside, a dark young man in a brown tunic and blue leggings took down the grey sail. Aidan ran to catch the painter and tie it to an iron ring. "I am Aidan mac Robert," he said eagerly, as the young man stepped ashore. "Do you have a message for me?"

The stranger gave Aidan a cool, appraising look, then his blue glance fell on me. His handsome features didn't flicker, but I felt like a worm squirming on the end of a spade. His eyes moved back to Aidan.

"I'm Bran mac Bru and my message is for Abbot Ninian," he said. "Will you take me to him?"

"Yes," nodded Aidan, and a friendly smile passed between them. As they strode away together up the path to the monastery, a buttery sun broke through the mist and stroked their shiny heads. Treading on Aidan's shadow, I scurried along behind.

It was evening, hours after Bran mac Bru had sailed away, before Abbot Ninian got round to sharing their conversation with the rest of us. Although too well trained to ask questions, the monks were pop-eyed with curiosity. Aidan had been practically out of his head since morning. Before the last prayer of the day, Abbot Ninian took pity on them all.

"As you know," he said in his unhurried way, "I had a

visitor today. He came from Earl Robert with two pieces of news." There was a provoking pause, during which I could hear Aidan panting like an excited puppy. In his own time, Abbot Ninian went on. "The day after tomorrow our friend Aidan will be leaving us to join the household of Earl Egfrid in Northumbria. Earl Robert will arrive before noon to fetch his son."

Not long ago, this information would have been greeted with sighs and murmurs of regret. Now that the monks were in the huff with Aidan, their response was muted. I avoided his eye and waited for the old man to get to the next point.

"Earl Robert has also sent the latest report on the movements of the Norsemen," he said.

At the word "Norsemen" a collective shiver, the nearest these private, repressed people ever came to a strong expression of emotion, seemed to make the candles dim. For all their belief in heaven, I thought contemptuously, at the prospect of death the monks were really no braver than rabbits. Except for Abbot Ninian, who continued coolly.

"The Norsemen have come further south during the summer. A week ago Earl Robert's spies saw dragon ships moored in the mouth of the river Tay, not thirty miles from here." The monks' eyes grew round in the dim light but, before they could even gasp, Abbot Ninian's voice went serenely on. "The good news is that they were taking on water and supplies, preparing for the voyage back to Norway. Our precautions will remain in place but –" a frosty smile twitched at the corners of the dry old mouth

"– it seems likely we shall sleep safely through the winter."

It was hardly long-term reassurance, but at least it was a reprieve.

"Thanks to God," mumbled the monks dutifully.

I whispered, "Time to go."

18

A Night to Remember

In the end, I didn't even have to lay a trap. I'd been awake all night, scratching flea-bites, tossing and turning as I tried to work out how to get Aidan where I wanted him and when. Should I be wistful: "Aidan, will you do something for me – since it's our last night together?" Should I pretend I'd had a sudden, mad idea: "Hey, listen, why don't we do something really exciting on your last night?" As it turned out, Aidan was as high as a kite and silly with it. I reckoned he was desperate to do something he could boast about to his new friends at Earl Egfrid's place. I could just see him, swaggering in a neat new tunic, being smart at my expense:

"You won't believe this! I've been living on a yucky island with my idiot brother and a bunch of grotty monks. Of course I didn't pay any attention to their silly rules. I've always done whatever I liked."

When he came giggling to my cell in the early morning, begging me to do exactly what I wanted him to do, I could scarcely believe my luck.

"I've had a great idea," he whispered, crawling into bed beside me and grabbing more than half of my blanket. "Tonight, when the monks are asleep, why don't we sneak away and spend the night together out of doors? We'll steal some food and have a midnight picnic. Share our last night talking and sleeping under the stars. What d'you say, Nic?"

What was there to say? I'd always thought Aidan was stupid, slow to read, plodding at Latin, incapable of singing a few notes in tune. But his greatest stupidity was to trust me. He actually believed, even after all the times I'd got him into trouble, that we'd part good friends. I was careful not to sound eager.

"I'm really not sure. There'll be a hell of a row if we're caught," I pointed out.

Aidan made a silly noise.

"We won't be caught. The monks sleep like the dead and provided we're back for morning prayer, they'll never know we've been away."

I went on playing hard to get.

"But supposing they did find out? Abbot Ninian would go absolutely spare. You may be going away tomorrow, but I'm not."

"I'll take responsibility," promised Aidan in a lordly fashion. "I'll say you protested but I insisted. Oh, come on,

Nic," he wheedled. "It's our last time together. Let's make it a night to remember."

It was hard not to laugh. It would be a night to remember, all right.

"How are we going to cook our supper? We won't be able to light a fire," I objected slyly. "We still have to take precautions because of the Norsemen."

Aidan was getting impatient.

"You heard what Abbot Ninian said last night. If the Norsemen were taking on water last week, they're gone by now. Anyway, we'll only need a tiny fire. Oh, say yes, Nic! Just to please me?"

How could I refuse to please my dear brother on his last night on the island? I kept him in suspense a little longer, then I said, "Well, all right."

"Great." Aidan was giggling again. "Remember to bring your blanket. You can leave the food-stealing to me."

"There's just one thing, Aidan."

"What?"

"I'm not spending an autumn night on the rocks at Largo Point. I know you don't feel the cold, but I'll freeze to death without some shelter. Let's go to the cave where the wood's kept, then we can get cosy."

"Whatever you like. It's just for fun."

Only it wasn't fun. Even if I hadn't been twisted with jealousy and planning to play a final, cruel trick on my brother, a midnight picnic on our last night would have been an emotionally overloaded affair. I had sung at evening prayer, automatically because by now I'd become bored by the simple, repetitive music. It was the words that made me shiver:

> *"The Lord watches over good people*
> *and listens to their cries,*
> *but he hates evil-doers.*
> *May their path be dark and slippery!*
> *May the Lord's angel strike them down!"*

No doubt comforting for the monks, who were still thinking of the murderous Norsemen. But not for me, who had just enough belief in God to make me afraid of him. As I crept away from the sleeping monastery and followed Aidan towards the cave, my deprived, loveless future confronted me like a black wall.

Perhaps the bleak words had depressed Aidan too, or perhaps he was belatedly feeling nostalgic. When we'd stumbled along the dark shore and were crouching over a little fire at the mouth of the cave, he was having to work hard to sound cheerful.

"Have a piece of trout, Nic, while I toast the cheese. And look – some good apples at last. Brother Coelman brought them from the monastery at Lindores when he went over last week to borrow their ram." I knew he was just gabbling to fill the silence. "I like sheep. I'll miss seeing the lambs born next spring."

I didn't bother to reply. By the time we'd finished eating and were sitting wrapped in our blankets by the glowing embers, melancholy had engulfed us. I was too sick and obsessed to change my intention but, as the moon rose eerily over the dark estuary, I was almost weeping with pain and loss.

Once I'd believed that nothing could separate Aidan and me. The very idea that we'd ever have a "last night together" would have seemed as improbable as it was nightmarish. But then I hadn't understood the rules of the world I lived in; the survival of the fittest, the rejection of the poor, the weak and the disabled. I couldn't have imagined how easily my kindly brother would accept that harsh reality.

"Are you cold, Nic? We could go back . . . "

"No, I'm fine. I'll just put some more wood on the fire."

I could hear the grating and stirring of the shingle as the tide ebbed below. The dragon-headed rock gleamed coldly in the moonlight and the causeway to the islet was like a shadow under the swirling water. A dark and slippery path would soon break the surface of the sea.

"Nic, I'm getting nervous about tomorrow."

"It's a bit late for that, isn't it?"

Obtuse to the end, Aidan had spent the whole day revelling in his good fortune.

"I've heard of Earl Egfrid. He's an ally of King Offa and very powerful. He has a great fortress near Alnwick . . . I'll have a white horse and ride every day over the hills . . . I

107

hope Father's bringing some decent clothes for me. I can't appear looking like this."

Now his thoughts had turned to the past.

"Do you remember the day we caught the squirrel, Nic? And the day we made the swing?" I remembered, and all the other occasions on which I'd been hurt and humiliated. "We had good times, didn't we? I do wish . . . "

"What?"

"That things could have turned out well for you, too. You won't forget me, will you?"

His sentimentality did me good. It hardened my heart.

"I won't forget you," I said evenly, "and you won't forget me, either."

"Of course not," said Aidan, reaching out to pat my knee. "Always friends."

He yawned and rolled over, pulling his blanket over his ears. I sat staring at the tall rock with its strange iron crown. The sea had shrunk further back and the causeway was gleaming in the moonlight like a long serpent's tail. I put more wood on the fire.

19

Meltdown

I'd meant to stay alert, but the fire was hot and I'd scarcely slept the previous night. Resting my head on the warm rock, I dropped down into the dark where not even dreams could reach me. When I started suddenly awake, the moon was riding high in a sky still black and sugared with stars. It was the tell-tale saffron line on the horizon that sent panic surging through me. How long had I been asleep? Had the fire gone out? *Had the tide turned?*

Despite the danger that my cherished plan had unravelled, I managed to keep cool. Glancing round, I saw Aidan curled up like a hedgehog in his rough blanket, and heard him snoring gently. There was still a faint glow in the heart of the fire. I could hear the hiss of the tide running in, but it hadn't reached the causeway. If I hurried, I could still make it. As I poked a long stick into the fire and bundled up my blanket, I ran over for the last time the moves I'd planned.

Take the burning stick and blanket and run down to the causeway. Dump the blanket on the grass and run out to the islet. Put up the ladder (the only difficult part, but there were crevices in the rock where I should be able to wedge the burning stick). Set fire to the brushwood in the basket (no need for oil, since the fuel would be like tinder after the long summer drought). Climb down and run back to the shore. Pick up the blanket. Sprint back to the monastery. Creep to my cell, shake out the blanket and muss up my bed. Then – "Father Ninian! Brother Ternan! Wake up! Aidan isn't in his cell. Oh, where can he be? Please come – I'm so frightened!"

I'd act distracted, whimpering and dashing from the cowshed to the writing-room, from the kitchen to the church. But I'd recover in time to join the search party. How could I miss seeing the monks' faces when they sighted the flaming basket, and found Aidan asleep, with the remains of his stolen supper by the fire? How could I miss seeing Aidan's face, as he was frogmarched back to explain himself to Father Ninian, not to mention Earl Robert a few hours later? It would be hilarious and, however Aidan might protest, there wouldn't be a shred of evidence to incriminate me.

The stick was sturdy and, when I withdrew it, the end burned brightly. It was still dark but, as I lifted my blanket and turned towards the shore, I saw the line on the horizon widening and turning pink. No time for gloating – I must hurry. An hour after sunrise, it would be time for morning prayer.

The causeway was wet and slippery under my sandalled feet. Normally I'd have been terrified of the incoming tide but, as I slithered along with my burning stick, I felt nothing but malicious glee. I lost time finding a crack wide and deep enough to hold the stick upright, but eventually I got it safely wedged. With strength I didn't know I had, I heaved up the ladder against the tall rock. Grabbing the stick, I climbed and pushed it in among the brittle twigs.

There was a delicate flicker like red lace, then a loud crackle and a mass of tiny flames. Before I'd even reached the ground the wood caught. Flames leapt and sparks flew into the sky. I was elated, but I had no time to admire the blaze. The tide was coming fast and I was at least fifteen minutes from the monastery. As I skipped towards the causeway, the eastern sky was rapidly paling – which was why, at the very last minute, every bloody thing went wrong. After four years as a monastery schoolboy, Aidan rose with the sun.

"Oi! What the hell are you doing, you evil little bastard?"

Before I had even set foot on the causeway, Aidan was at the other end. As he leapt towards me with the sea swishing about his feet, his face was like a lurid mask. I saw his muscular shoulders flexing, his strong hands tensed like claws. I had a wild thought of jumping into the water, but the tide was whirling in ominous little pools and I wasn't a strong swimmer. While I hesitated, Aidan reached the islet. As he sprang forward, he was howling with rage.

"You filthy piece of trash! I'll give you the thrashing of your dirty little life."

Screaming with terror, I backed away from him, squirming into the space between the ladder and the rock. Fragments of burning wood were falling around me, hissing like snakes as they touched the wet algae at the water's edge.

"I'm sorry. I'm sorry. Don't hit me, Aidan!"

My pleas were drowned by the roaring of the fire, but they'd have been unheeded anyway. Aidan's lips were drawn back in a snarl and his eyes glinted vengefully. Would he have beaten me to pulp? I'll never know. As he reached out to knock the ladder aside, my hands closed on the rungs. Strengthened by sheer terror, I pushed it straight at him.

Everything happened quickly after that. Probably blind rage had slowed Aidan's reactions; when the ladder crashed down, he didn't get out of the way fast enough to avoid a glancing blow. While he winced and clasped his shoulder, I rocketed forward and headbutted him hard in the stomach. As he doubled up, he caught his foot on the ladder and stumbled sideways onto the slimy rock. I saw his eyes popping and his arms flailing as he skidded and teetered, then he just slithered into the sea.

"Nic! Help me! Push out the ladder!" I could hear Aidan's voice, shrill with terror, above the noise of the fire. I could see his wet head bobbing on the blood-red water, chin up as he battled against the powerful undertow. I could see his fingers, like stunted tentacles, scrabbling at the sharp, barnacled rocks. "For the love of God, Nic! Help me!"

I swear I never meant to kill him. All I'd wanted was to watch him suffer as I had; to see him withering in the blast of his father's anger, to see him start his swanky new life with his good guy's reputation in rags. I wanted him to know the pain and despair of being me. Only when I saw him drowning, the most poisonous of thoughts came into my mind. If Aidan were dead, there would be no witness to my wicked deed, *and I would be my father's heir*. In a flash of evil desire I visualised myself not as a verminous, rheumaticky monk, sentenced to hard labour for life, but as a young lord in a fur cloak and embroidered tunic, riding on a white horse over the hills.

"Nic! Please, push out the ladder . . . "

I didn't move. Coldly I watched my brother's fingers wilt and slide into the water. I saw his mouth gaping as the tide whirled him away. His head resurfaced twice before it vanished under the waves.

For a moment I felt nothing, then suddenly my stomach contracted. Leaning forward I vomited, throwing up sour fish and apple and bits of cheese. Yet even as I spluttered and wiped my mouth, I was starting to rehearse my explanation to Abbot Ninian and my father.

"Believe me, Father. I didn't want a midnight picnic, but Aidan was determined and what could I say? It was our last night together, after all. Of course, when I realised he wanted to light the fire in the basket I was shocked – but you know what a silly mood he's been in recently. I tried to talk him out of it, honestly, but he was determined. He said –" pause for some sobbing here "– that it would give the monks something to remember him by. I only went onto the islet to try to stop him, but I couldn't – he was so much stronger than me. He was hitting me when he slipped and fell in the water. I did my best to save him – I tried to grab his hand and I even pushed out the ladder, but it was no use. The tide was so strong . . . Oh, Father, I'll miss him so much . . ."

Would Abbot Ninian and Earl Robert have fallen for this load of bull? Another question without an answer. As I scrambled away from the place where Aidan had died, my eye was unexpectedly caught by a movement out in the estuary. As I stared, I again tasted acid and my body began to shake violently. Against the orange sunrise, four square-sailed longships were moving swiftly upriver. The Norsemen had not gone home.

"My God, rescue me from wicked men, from the power of cruel and evil ones . . . "

Too late for prayer; the monks' worst nightmare was about to come true. Scarcely noticing the scorching heat, I squirmed on my belly across the smoky lichen to the tall rock. Sobbing and fearing for my life, I cowered there – I who had just watched my brother drown.

The hideous, gaping dragon faces rushed towards the island along the path of the rising sun. I heard the swish of the churning water and the creak of the striped canvas sails. I saw the shipped oars, the glint of iron helmets and the rows of brightly painted shields. They were so close, I thought I was lost, but no one even noticed me. The longships, saved from the rocks by the light I'd wickedly provided, slipped round the side of the island and disappeared.

My relief was indecent, but also short-lived. As I got up shakily, I saw the shadow rise with me in the pale sunlight. There was something puzzling about it; a moment elapsed before I realised what it was. For the first time ever, it was attached to a body – mine. In the blood-frozen pause between the tramp of feet and the screams, Nic Moonlight surfaced and the horrible truth dawned. The shadow that had lured me to this terrible place, and that now seemed to be clamped to my feet wasn't, and never had been Aidan's. It was Neacal's.

In a frenzy of denial I howled my real name: *"Nicholas Moonlight!"* and, as if an echo had answered, I remembered what to do. With trembling hands, I untied the strings of my leather bag. Riffling through stale food scraps, I found the stump of candle I'd kept long after I'd forgotten what it was for. As the glowing fire above my head caved in, showering the islet with red-hot ash, I knelt and set it alight.

"Oh, Mum! Oh, Dad," I whispered, as I extinguished the tiny flame.

20

The Seagull

In the time it takes to blink, I was back in my bedroom, but any thankfulness I felt was just as brief. The moon was still shining on the wall where I'd last seen the shadow, and I knew that at any moment I might see it again. As I kicked off my trainers and dived under the duvet, I cursed my smug certainty that the shadow was Aidan's; that a nice, kind boy was inviting me to be his friend. What a dork I'd been, letting myself be fooled by the twinny similarity of skirted tunic and long bare legs. As I tucked the duvet round me, desperate to exclude every chink of light, I knew I was in deadly danger – and that I didn't have a lot of time.

I was sure he would come for me again, the restless, resentful spirit who'd conjured up music, taken possession of my mind and involved me in dreadful crimes. Even if I could summon enough courage and willpower to resist touching him, there was nothing to stop him touching me. He could get me here, or at home in Edinburgh, at school or on the street; wherever the sun or moon shone on the earth. He wasn't going to go away.

Rigid with fear, I visualised my next trip back in time. Would the Norsemen have left the island, leaving me to crawl back along the causeway and find the gentle monks horribly slain? Or would I be seen by the raiders and have my own throat cut? One of these things must surely have happened to Neacal.

Suddenly, it mattered terribly to me to know what my frightful alter ego's end had been. If my fate was to share it, I must try to be braver than I'd ever been. But if I knew in advance, I just might be able to take avoiding action and break out of this devilish enchantment. Clutching at a straw? Yes, but as Father Lochran once said in church, hope is the last thing that dies.

Only who could possibly know the fate of one twelve-year-old boy who had lived more than a thousand years ago? There was just one possibility – maybe a chance in a million, but this was a desperate time.

Cautiously I lifted the edge of the duvet and peeped out. A merciful cloud had drifted over the moon, so I got out of bed. My door was open and so was Dad's; I could make him out as I passed, hunched like a walrus under the bedclothes. Tiptoeing downstairs, I slipped into the kitchen. Dad had left the computer switched on; its blue screen glowed like a huge jewel in the darkened room. I sat down, groped for the mouse and clicked on, then I entered Auntie Sadie's e-mail address. This is the message I keyed in:

"VERY URGENT
"*Dear Mum*
"*Dad says you know a lot about the island long ago. Did you ever hear of two boys called Aidan and Neacal? Their father was called Earl Robert and they may have lived in the 8th century. Do you know what happened to Neacal? It's important, so please e-mail back ASAP.*"

Then, as loneliness and longing for home brought tears to my eyes, I added:

"*I miss you. Love, Nic*".

I clicked the send button but, as I left the kitchen, a feeling of futility swept over me. The grandfather clock said five to one. I was pretty sure that, by the time Mum got up at half-past seven, it would be too late.

In a way, I was both right and wrong. I wasn't destined to go back to the monastery – but Neacal mac Robert certainly hadn't finished with me. When I got upstairs, the moon was again shining across my floor, but there was no sign of the shadow. Completely shattered, I got into bed and passed out cold.

I don't know how long I'd slept but, when I awoke, I

could almost smell Neacal. The moon had disappeared and my room felt damp, as if sea mist had come indoors and wrapped itself round the furniture and me. When I felt an icy hand groping under the duvet, I moaned in horror, but when bony fingers encircled my wrist I was too frightened to scream.

"Get up," commanded a thin voice that I knew was Neacal's.

I obeyed as automatically as I had touched his shadow. In deep darkness I drifted downstairs and out into the yard. There the moon was so bright, it was like a searchlight shining into my face. As the unseen hand pulled me away from the cottage, down onto the shore path, I realised that Neacal's shadow was no longer attached to my feet. As my eyes adjusted, I could see my frail moonshadow stumbling along beside his black one, clamped by his fingers on my wrist. But the only body on the path was mine.

"Please, let me go," I pleaded, trying to pull my hand away. I might have been handcuffed with a ring of steel.

"Keep walking," ordered Neacal in his thin ghost's voice.

The tide was on the turn. Limping along the stony path in my thin socks, I could see water running like mercury over the fluorescent shore. As we rounded the island and I saw the black serpent of causeway and rock, I began to cry.

"Why are you doing this?" I sobbed. "Are you going to drown me?"

I heard Neacal laugh mirthlessly.

"Oh, yes," he said. "That's how I get rid of people –

remember? But this time I'm going to keep hold of you. Can't have you slipping away, when I need your body so much."

"*My body?*"

Again I heard his tinny laugh.

"Of course. I got into your mind easily enough, but you didn't think I'd stop there, did you? It's no fun being a mind without a body, and that's what I've been for more years than you can imagine. Pity about your deafness, but otherwise your body will suit me perfectly. Your parents won't know the difference, and I'm sure they'll be much kinder than mine ever were."

As the full implication of these words dawned on me, I began to scream.

"Help! Help! Somebody help me!"

Neacal laughed again.

"Howl as much as you like," he said indifferently. "I howled too. Nobody hears."

He was so confident, but he was wrong. As I was dragged to the wet causeway and propelled remorselessly onto the islet where Aidan had died, I heard a harsh cry overhead. As if a lock had sprung open, my arm was released and I saw the shadow skittering wildly about. Looking up in the cold moonlight, I saw a seagull hurtling over the cliff. In a blatter of white wings, it swooped towards the islet, its powerful claws snatching furiously at the shadow.

Cowering on the water's edge, I saw the monstrous thing lifted and shaken as if it was a scrap of blanket. Thrown down again, it lay hissing and writhing like a wounded snake. Then the seagull struck in earnest. Tearing and shredding with its curved beak and claws, it ripped the shadow to thin black fragments. I thought I heard wailing as they drifted like soot into the sea.

The dawn was coming up as the seagull perched on top of the rock, watching me with its cold, speculative eye. Only when it saw Dad running along the causeway through the incoming tide did it rise, circle over my head and fly straight out to sea.

21

e-mail

I've only the vaguest recollection of Dad wrapping a blanket round me, picking me up and carrying me home. I remember having a hot bath and putting on my pyjamas. I remember not being able to hear a thing and not caring. I got into bed, closed my eyes over Dad's anxious face and fell thankfully asleep.

When I woke, the first thing I saw was that an armchair had been placed by the window. A magazine and a book lay beside it, but there was no sign of Dad. I was puzzled to notice the sun slanting into the room; the front of the cottage faced north-west, so the sun never shone on it until early evening. I was sitting up when Dad pushed open the door and came in with what I thought was my breakfast on a tray.

"Six o'clock. Time for tea in bed," he said.

S-I-CK-Z O-K-L-O-K. T-EE I-N B-E-D. No wonder I was starving.

122

"What's to eat?" I asked.

"Ham and egg pie." H-A-M A-N-D E-G P-EY.

"I'm glad it's not fish," I remarked, as Dad put the tray across my knees. "No kidding, I'm sick of fish."

He gave me an odd look, but he didn't ask me to explain. Pointing to a folded sheet of paper on the tray, he said, "An e-mail from Mum came through. I printed it out for you. I expect you know what it's about."

I nodded, then I said curiously, "Dad – how did you know where I was?"

"I didn't," he replied. "I got up to go to the loo and saw your bed was empty. I'd been all over the effing island before I found you." Dad isn't a swearing man and I could see he was still badly shaken. "I think we'll have to talk to Dr MacGrouther about this sleepwalking, Nic," he warned. "He'll probably want to change your pills."

He left the room abruptly, so I had to shelve telling him what Dr MacGrouther could do with his pills. I'd had some experience of addiction, and knew how it could bend your mind, making you hear voices that weren't there and do things you didn't want to do. It was terrifying and I'd never risk getting hooked on drugs, even ones shelled out at the health centre. I cut my ham and egg pie into bite-sized pieces and ate them with my fingers while I read what Mum had to say.

"*Dear Nic*"

Nic? That was an unexpected though welcome start.

"*Thank you for your e-mail. Yes, I do recognise the names*

Aidan and Neacal. Some people would tell you that they're only characters in a legend, though I think myself they probably did exist. I first heard the story when I was a child and we lived for a year on a farm north of Dundee called Munlichte – a strange coincidence, since the surname 'Moonlight' is a form of 'Munlichte' and Dad's family came originally from the same area. The story goes that, once upon a time, a Scottish lord, Earl Robert Munlichte, had twin sons called Aidan and Neacal."

So there was some connection between the red-headed twins and me, I thought in amazement. Although they had been known only as "sons of Robert", away back in the mists of time their family had been Moonlights too. I read on eagerly.

"Aidan had all the fairy-tale gifts. He was handsome, loyal and brave, while Neacal was cunning and ugly."

Yes, I agreed, it did sound like a fairy tale, but it was also an accurate description of the boys I'd known.

"Neacal was jealous of Aidan and wished him dead so that he could inherit his father's lands. When the boys were sent to be educated at a monastery, the monks sent them one day to catch fish on an island nearby. While Aidan was fishing from a rock, Neacal pushed him into the sea."

I could see where this was coming from, but one thing was for sure. My version was a hell of a lot more dramatic.

"Up to this point," Mum continued, *"there's probably some truth in the story – but then it becomes completely fantastical. Neacal, it's said, was haunted by his drowned brother in the form of a seagull. Wherever he looked, the seagull was there, watching him."*

I could feel my eyes popping and I nearly choked on my ham and egg pie.

"Eventually Neacal's guilt became too much to bear. He broke down and confessed to his abbot. His penance was to renounce his claim to the lands of Munlichte and become a hermit. He lived alone in a cave, and the abbot gave him the job of lighting a fire to warn seafarers of hidden rocks."

It was like a distorted echo of the truth, this account. You could see where bits like the Viking raid had been forgotten and where other bits had been invented to fit the storyline. Only I could make an educated guess at Neacal's true fate. He'd become a hermit because he was the sole survivor of the Viking raid. I shuddered at the thought of his lonely, haunted existence – for the seagull, whether Mum considered it fantastical or not, was real. Not only had it rid the island of an evil spirit, but it had watched over me and saved my life.

"When I was young," Mum had written, *"I thought the story was entirely a legend – European folklore is full of similar tales. So I was surprised, when I was studying archaeology at university, to find a few fragments of historical evidence connecting Aidan and Neacal to Seagull Island. The name of the islet 'Inchaed' means 'Aidan's Isle', and there are marks on the tall rock that suggest there was once some sort of container bolted onto it. Archaeologists think it may have been a primitive lighthouse."*

Interesting, but not perturbing. The next bit was seriously spooky, though.

"In the 1930s, a carved stone (now in the Gleeport Museum) surfaced on the beach on Seagull Island – quite near the cottage, as it happens. Only part of the inscription was still legible, the letters EACA MONACHU. Historians think it originally said, NEACAL MONACHUS, which is Latin for 'Neacal the Monk'. Underneath there's a cross with a line drawn through it, which suggests that by the time he carved it, the monk had lost his Christian faith."

As I read these words, I felt quite woozy for a minute or two. Only then it occurred to me that seeing a stone that wasn't there was hardly the weirdest thing that had happened to me on Seagull Island. And Mum's explanation confirmed something I already knew about Neacal mac Robert of Munlichte – that he had very little faith to lose. Forced against his will to be a monk, he'd only found life half tolerable as long as he could sing.

I remembered painfully how he'd despised the monks for being afraid of the Vikings, as if having a normal human fear of a violent death made them hypocrites. I had an intense, poignant memory of old Abbot Ninian, with his brave eyes and humorous mouth; of gentle Brother Coelman, who called his sheep "my children"; of young, earnest Brother Ternan, muttering, "Bless the bread, bless the soup," as he went about his chores. They had believed in God, all right, and I hoped they'd found the heaven they were looking for.

Now that she'd told her story, Mum went straight into mumlike mode.

"That's all I can tell you, Nic, and I don't know if it's helpful.

I don't want to be a fussy mummy, but it's worrying when your son sends you an urgent e-mail in the middle of the night — especially since your silly Auntie Sadie keeps banging on about Seagull Island being haunted. If there's something wrong, please tell Dad immediately. I miss you too. Love, Mum".

I ate the last piece of pie and wiped my fingers on the duvet, then I went and pulled down my rucksack from the top of the wardrobe. When I'd folded the e-mail and put it in a zipped pocket, I took the tray downstairs to the kitchen. Dad was standing at the worktop, making himself a mug of coffee. He turned and smiled at me.

"I'd like to go home now," I said.

"Good. Me too," he replied.

It was the following afternoon when the *Spirit of Fife* carried us over to Gleeport on our way home. I'd slept in Dad's bed last night, and tonight I would sleep in my own. I was standing on the quay waiting for Dad and Andy to heave our boxes and suitcases ashore when I saw an absolutely amazing sight. Galloping down the cobbled street opposite was a golden retriever puppy with Mum on the end of a leash. Mum was practically taking off but it was the dog that was going places — like to a lamppost outside the Gleeport Hotel. As I watched open-mouthed, it careered three times round the post before triumphantly cocking its leg. As Mum battled to unwind the leash, I ran towards her. I was laughing my head off and so was she.

22

The Isle of the Shadow

I hope no one reading this story imagined that, at the end, I'd miraculously get my hearing back. There was never a snowball's chance in hell of that. I'm sixteen now and I'm completely deaf, though I believe in every other way I'm happier and more normal than I was before my illness. Having the dog (Mufty Moonlight) helped; he's really cool and naturally it's never mattered to him that I'm deaf. But, paradoxically, it was my fearsome experience on Seagull Island that booted me from headbanging delinquency into a healthier frame of mind.

There are differences of opinion in the family about what actually happened to me that strange, moony summer four years ago. Auntie Sadie says it was a proper haunting by proper ghosts, and it's a wonder I escaped alive. She's stopped chucking gravel at seagulls when they crap on her washing in the back garden, and she throws out bread for them, just in case one of them is Aidan. But, as I've already mentioned, Auntie Sadie isn't like anyone else.

I've never talked much to Dad about the weeks we spent together on the island. Although the idea of me sleepwalking bothered him plenty, he found it even harder to accept that my being on Inchaed that last night had an occult explanation. He's a scientist, after all. I know he still worries that he didn't look after me properly – as if he could possibly have saved me from anything so offbeat. I feel protective, because grown-ups aren't as tough as kids.

It's different with Mum. When I came back from the island, she and I both had some proper counselling, which was useful, though we gave it up after we'd remembered how to talk to each other. In the evenings, when Dad's been away in Japan or Australia or wherever, I've told her most of what happened. She's a good listener and she's never suggested I was imagining things. She has suggested, though, that what happened was probably an experience in my mind. She thinks my knowledge of Aidan and Neacal is evidence of some thought-transference between herself and me. For a while, I had no problem with this, because the most scary bit of what happened to me was to share Neacal mac Robert's twisted mind. More recently, I've come back to believing that Seagull Island is haunted in a more general way.

To be honest, I have mixed feelings about Neacal. OK, the guy was a sad case. He was one of nature's ugly bugs and his parents had completely messed up his short life. That doesn't alter the fact that by the time my mind tangled with his, he was a mean, petulant little pig. He was totally self-obsessed and he took out his frustration on the one person who – however thickly tactless – had shown him tolerance and affection.

So, who does that remind you of? What real difference is there between putting a slowworm in someone's bed and throwing mud balls at someone's knickers hanging on the rotary-drier? The only difference is that I didn't have access to a slowworm. I know Neacal didn't intend his final outrage to end the way it did; he didn't set out to kill his brother. His brother died, just the same. When I set fire to my birthday tea, I didn't mean to injure my parents, but either of them might have been badly burned.

There's no way of knowing how Neacal mac Robert might have developed if he'd had good parents like mine. Maybe if Earl Robert hadn't called him "Weasel" and made such a fuss of Aidan, Neacal wouldn't have hated them both so much. If his mother had shown Neacal affection and talked up his confidence, he might have come to terms with the way he looked – we can't all be drop-dead hunky, after all. All I know is that, by the time I left the island, I didn't ever want to be like him.

I've written my story down because, as I get older and exam pressure builds, I might forget – and anyway, it's time to move on. My life can never be the way I once imagined it, but I think it's pretty cool. I suppose if I'd gone to St Augustine's I'd have made friends, though they'd also have been rivals – show me the performer who doesn't want to be a star. And although a bit of me will always grieve for the music I loved so much, I have far more real friends than I'd ever have had as a young prodigy. I swim and go to the gym and, since at last I've grown to a reasonable size, I have karate lessons and do a bit of cross-country. I even play squash with big Gerald Slade. He's improved a lot with age and says he only made moon jokes when we were kids for the pleasure of seeing my pouty wee face.

On Saturday nights I go dancing at the youth club with my mates. I can't hear the music, but I can feel the beat, and when no one can hear a word anyone else is saying, I interpret for them. Dad asked me recently if I'd like a drum kit, but I said no. It was a kind thought, but if you've ever played Bach's partitas on the violin, I doubt you'd get much joy knocking hell out of a piece of animal skin.

I've never wanted to go back to Seagull Island, and I know I never will. I couldn't sleep in the room where once I was haunted by the shadow. I couldn't fish from the pier or bear to look at the bleak islet where Aidan died. Mum and Dad feel the same, and they're talking about buying a timeshare in Spain.

Yet sometimes still, when I look out of my window and see the moon rising over the dark roofs of Edinburgh, it all comes back so vividly – the glassy sun reflecting in the rock pools, the swirl of seabirds and the great grey estuary flowing out to the

131

sea. I hear voices singing inside my head, and sheep calling to their lambs on the green hillside. In my mind's eye I see the pious monks who heard God's voice in lonely places, and two doomed children playing noughts and crosses on the sand.

I've wondered sometimes whether I was the only person ever to have a spooky experience on Seagull Island. Had the ghost of Neacal Munlichte tried to steal other bodies, or did he recognise the name "Nicholas Moonlight" as his own? Now, though I'll never be able to compare notes with anyone else, I think I know the answer to that question. One night recently, I was revising for my economics exam. Quite late, Mum wandered into my bedroom in her dressing-gown, with her reading glasses half way down her nose. She was carrying a book and looking slightly fazed.

"Nic," she said, putting the book down open on my desk, "promise me you'll never tell Sadie about this. I'd hate to hear her crowing, 'I told you so.'"

"About what?"

Mum wrinkled her nose and ran her hand through her greying hair.

"It says here," she told me, "that the name 'Seagull Island' has nothing to do with seagulls. It's a corruption of an old Gaelic name, *Eilean na Sgàile*."

In the light of my Anglepoise lamp, I looked where her finger was pointing.

"*Eilean na Sgàile*," I read. "The Isle of the Shadow".

THE END